Yet Another
Death in Venice

Yet Another Death in Venice

A Simon Bognor Mystery

TIM HEALD

MYSTERIOUSPRESS.COM

OPEN ROAD
INTEGRATED MEDIA
NEW YORK

Cover design by Neil Alexander Heacox

978-1-4804-6828-3

Published in 2014 by MysteriousPress.com/Open Road Integrated Media, Inc.
345 Hudson Street
New York, NY 10014
www.mysteriouspress.com
www.openroadmedia.com

For Michael Dibdin,
who once made my ears bleed briefly
during the Semana Negra *in Gijón,*
northern Spain; and for K. K. Beck,
who met him there and took him away to Seattle.

Yet Another
Death in Venice

1

A thin sleet-laden wind blew in from the Dolomites and drove the orchestras outside the Quadri and the Florian out of the piazza and into the warmth of their respective establishments. All around the great square, tiny white horses frothed above the little waves that beat against the duckboards. All along the Riva degli Schiavoni in front of the Doge's Palace and the facades of the grand hotels— the Danieli, the Savoia e Jolanda, the Londra Palace, the Metropole, and all the other hostelries where John Ruskin and Henry James and others less literate but just as famous might have stayed from time to time—the gray-white gale banged the gondolas and the vaporetti against the stone of the wide esplanade.

None of this wintry weather, however, diminished the enthusiasm of the crowds that thronged the walkways or splashed in vividly colored boots through the sometimes knee-high water. It was Carnival time in Venice, and the crowds who gathered every year at the end of January and the beginning of February were as festive and foreign as ever. Carnival had ancient Venetian antecedents, but they were essentially bogus and dated from long before living memory.

Irving G. Silverburger had been in Venice for a week capitalizing on the success of his movie *The Coffee Grinders* and trying to drum up support for a sequel along the lines of *The Nut Crackers*, *The Lemon Peelers*, *The Meat Mincers*, or something similar. Irving G. Silverburger was not into art, but he was into money. And in some parts of the world, *The Coffee Grinders* was big box office. Celluloid garbage was by way of being Silverburger's stock in trade. Not, of course, that Silverburger was his real name. His family came from one of the Baltic states, and uncles and aunts had perished in concentration camps. These facts he rolled out when it suited him, which was not always.

He was staying at the Danieli. One did. In a penthouse suite. Likewise. And he paid his bill on his new pink credit card, the one that entitled him to "free" champagne more or less anywhere he went. The desk at the Danieli seemed not to have seen a pink card before and did not respond as he would have wished even when he explained that "pink was the new black." Nevertheless, he paid on the card, and they eventually accepted it. One did that, too, but not everyone seemed to realize.

Outside, he shivered in the winter air and brushed imaginary stuff off the lapels of his vicuna coat. It was yesterday's coat, but vicuna had a timeless sense of money about it, and he liked to give off that kind of scent. He sniffed the salty aroma of the Dolomites and the Adriatic and wondered if it could be bottled.

The city was becoming more and more like a film set. Silverburger liked that. The nearest he could think of was Vegas, but the trouble with Vegas was that it wasn't, you know, real. It was a fabrication—artificial. The great thing about Venice was that it was the real thing, like those ruins in Mexico and Guatemala. Only Venice had electricity and Wi-Fi, and you could get a dry martini and a burger, even if it was only in Harry's Bar and only if you specially ordered it, but what the hell. And no cars was good, too. Cars got in the way. They were always there when you didn't need them, whereas even a rusty old vaporetto gave you atmosphere, and atmosphere was what movies were about. Besides which, no one ever got run down by a vaporetto.

The city created its own special effects, and fewer and fewer people actually lived there. That was good, too. Citizens created nuisance. That was why New York and Paris and London were so difficult. People lived there. People got in the way.

He sighed and looked around. He bet none of these revelers came from Venice. The few Venetians left would be indoors minding their cats. Because nearly all the Carnival spirits were in masks, it was difficult to be sure of anything. Most of the masks had long noses and came, he guessed, from Taiwan or Guangzhou, the former Canton. These were the new homes of cheap junk just as Manchester and even parts of his home country had once been. Sure as hell, the masks wouldn't have been made in Venice any more than the wearers. Everything was from out of town.

He sighed and patted his breast pocket, the one where he had stored the pink plastic. The knowledge that the card was there reassured him. It confirmed his place in the world and gave him status. This was important in contemporary Venice. It earned him his table of choice at Locanda Cipriani and Corte Sconta and Al Covo and the Met. He scored points as he sauntered nonchalantly across the piazza or paid a quick genuflectory visit to the Frari to pay homage to the Titian altarpiece or to the Scuola Grande di San Rocco to make a speedy obeisance before the Tintoretto crucifixion on the first floor. Just because Silverburger made his fortune from junk didn't mean that he dealt in junk when left to his own devices.

Somewhere in the distance, an orchestra was playing Vivaldi. Someone was always playing Vivaldi in Venice. The composer had become a sort of permanent sound bite to be performed to a visual counterpoint provided by Guardi or Canaletto. Venice was a city of clichés, instantly recognizable to anyone who ever went to the cinema and saw an advertisement for ice cream.

He guessed there were packages for Carnival. Nowadays,

Venice came almost only in sanitized, gift-wrapped form, prepackaged so that you could march through the city in a bedraggled crocodile behind a drooping flag carried at half-mast by a tour leader almost as ignorant as those they were allegedly guiding. Venice was an experience you purchased on the Internet and saw through the prism of a digital camera. Silverburger had seen boatloads of a new phenomenon—mainland Chinese, coated apparently in nothing but plastic, being harangued in shrill Mandarin as they bucketed down the Giudecca Canal. It was not a pretty sound bite, but it was the noise of the future. Better stay at home and experience Venice vicariously on the screen. There wasn't a whole lot of difference between the big wrap-around screen of the downtown cinema in Middle America and the small screen of a handheld camera. The former, however, swelled the Silverburger coffers and improved the viability of the pink card in his suit pocket. Irving was a rich man and was becoming better off by the nanosecond.

His water taxi was late. He had ordered his own boat not wishing to risk sharing with someone else, which was always a hazard with the hotel vessel even though the desk had assured him that no one else was making the voyage out to Marco Polo. He preferred his own taxi. You could order the boatman about, whereas the Danieli fellow served another master. Or thought he did.

Silverburger gazed at the throng wondering idly how many were mainland Chinese and how many were likely to be the bums on seats watching *The Coffee Grinders* and films of that ilk in downtown Peoria. He shrugged and shivered despite the vicuna coat and a silk vest next the skin. Came to the same thing. There were plenty of bums in mainland China and a similar appetite for bad movies. There was a fortune to be made out of the lowest common denominator, and Silverburger was making it.

His taxi slid and bumped along, skippered by a helmsman in a white peaked cap wearing a truculent grin and wraparound shades. Silverburger smiled an unspoken reply and watched the bellhop load his designer luggage onto the boat. He tipped him in paper Euros and stepped on board. The boat rocked slightly and thumped against the side as he made his way back and sat in the stern, arms akimbo, trying to disguise the shivering reaction to the cold and to look like the self-assured American film mogul that he surely was.

The taxi driver gunned the engine, and he and the passenger waved a nonchalant farewell to the grand hotel as they slipped down the tributary and into the approaches to the Grand Canal. Silverburger had seldom seen such crowds so assiduously disguised. There was not a recognizable human face among them, and all wore costumes. It was like Halloween back home, only a sight more conscientious.

He did not observe the Harlequin figure straddling the balustrade on the bridge and smoking a cigarette through a holder as it toyed with a wonderfully realistic crossbow in its arms. Had he done so, he would have paid the Harlequin little or no attention, for it was just one of many thousands of similarly disguised figures mostly vaporettoed in from the bus and train stations by the new bridge that traversed the canal up at the Piazzale Roma that connected with the concrete jungle of Mestre and the real world beyond.

Here, all was make-believe. The cavorting revelers, the Pinocchio-style noses, the frantic and often down-turned mouths, the crinolines, the breeches, the wigs, the hats. All would be translated in a day or two into sensible suiting and polished shoes. These few days of fantasy would be restored to the daily slog and the hourly grind. Silverburger, on the other hand, was all fiction and no fact. This sort of fabrication, tatty and tawdry though it might be, was what he did day in and day out. Even this routine water taxi trip out to the airport and the executive lounge before the fast-track progress into first class was part of the unreal world he inhabited. His life was as artificial as the means by which it was supported.

Death, too. There was to be nothing routine or ordinary in the departure of Irving G. Silverburger dispatched by the effective bolt of the crossbow wielded by the anonymous Harlequin on the bridge. One minute, the slim androgynous mildly eighteenth-century figure bent sinuously almost as if playing a character from a Goldoni play, egged on by music from Vivaldi played by the competing orchestras of the Quadri and the Florian on opposite sides of the busy piazza; the next, the bolt had fled toward the departing launch and embedded itself in the coat-clad back of the film producer from Middle America.

Undeterred, the gleaming mahogany launch chugged up the Grand Canal. She passed the Picassos and other modern treasures at Peggy Guggenheim's place; the Tintorettos in the Accademia. She moved under the clogged bric-a-brac of the Rialto Bridge, a commission that Palladio had so signally failed to win, and ignored the empty windswept stalls of the fish and vegetable markets on the left before taking in the crumbling facade of the majestic Ca' d'Oro with its one beardy Van Dyck and its obligatory Carpaccio of Saint George once more dispatching the dragon. All was real and yet not real.

On the open lagoon, the driver opened up, gunning his engine to new strengths and leaving behind a wake that overwhelmed the white flecks from the short wavelets fanned by the wind from the distant mountains.

Thus they sped across the waters. An incoming cut-price flight passed them overhead, passengers buckled up and prepared to bulk the existing crowds of tourists with instant disguises and sudden anonymity. In the stern of the craft, Silverburger sat motionless in his overcoat, arms akimbo still as he stared out unseeing on the world outside the water taxi.

At their destination, the driver casually bumped his craft into the jetty, did arcane yet unthinking things with ropes, and only then turned to assist his passenger from the boat.

Silverburger was sitting as he had sat since setting off from the Danieli a half hour before. Indeed, he seemed not to have moved at all despite the motion of the vessel and the cold of the clime.

The captain called out in a rough Venetian dialect, which Silverburger would not have understood even though he might have recognized the message, which was simply that the journey was at an end and the money due. The client didn't move, and Giuseppe swore roughly, checked that the ropes were holding steady, and made his way toward the back. Once in the stern section of the boat, he spoke again to his passenger and, on receiving no answer, grasped Silverburger by his Manhattan-tailored shoulder and was surprised when the man fell forward, limp and unprotesting. In the small of his back there was a neat hole from which there protruded the end of a metal bolt. All around the point of entry, there was a widening smudge of fresh blood. This represented the final ebb of what had once been the life force, in a manner of speaking, of the blood's owner, or perhaps more accurately, of its leaseholder, Mr. Irving G. Silverburger.

Giuseppe swore again. Not because he was distressed by what he saw, but because corpses did not tend to carry cash. Not that it mattered. In any case, Mr. Silverburger dealt in plastic, and most recently in the pink plastic, which so few people in Italy seemed to recognize.

He was, of course, extremely dead.

2

Michael Dibdini was not actually head of police in Venice, but he probably knew more of the city and the crimes therein than any man alive. He was not a Venetian himself and came, like so many who dwelled in the city and had made their lives there, from somewhere else. It was said that his mother was English, his father Greek, and that his name was neither Michael nor Dibdini, but this seemed not to matter. He was a doge among men, a God among the *gondolieri*, and when it came to crime in La Serenissima, he was the ultimate authority. He also understood *fegato*, polenta, very small fish, and prosecco served in thin, chilled flutes with bubbles that rose from bottom to top only to disappear as mysteriously and totally as they had begun their brief voyage. They vanished as they had started: silently, unobtrusively, inevitably, and without trace. Just, Dibdini sometimes reflected, like a decomposed body surfacing in the secretive waters that surrounded the walls of his adopted city.

Dibdini was a friend of Sir Simon Bognor.

Their paths had first crossed when Her Majesty the Queen had come on a visit and Bognor had arrived as a typically British visitor on what he described in his inimitably clipped old-fashioned accent as a "recky." A man from the palace wearing a suit and by secretaries who wore twin sweater sets and sardonic smiles that suggested mischief had accompanied him. However, this was kept, sadly, under wraps. The man from the palace wore his suit as if born to it. It fit. Bognor's didn't. He appeared oddly uncomfortable in it, and it did not seem, as it did with so many Englishmen of his background, like a second skin. It seemed not to belong to him but to have been acquired from some sort of secondhand shop worn originally by some other person altogether. Dibdini, who was trained to notice such things, noticed. Even had he not been trained, he would still have noticed. Dibdini was that sort of man; Bognor's sartorial uncomfortableness spoke of an inner misfit, which Dibdini recognized at once.

The two men were oddly similar and from this shared round-peggedness masquerading in such square holes came a natural affinity and eventually a wary friendship.

And now Bognor was "Sir Simon," and he was in Venice for a day or so with Lady Bognor and he was proposing lunch, for old time's sake, at La Locanda Montin in what passed for the garden. They would eat a *fritto misto*, drink a carafe of the house white, and the years would slip easily away. They always had a meal at Montin, which was fashionable in a faded way and had entertained the likes of Henry Kissinger in their pomp, which might have been off-putting except that no one cared. This was one of the reasons that both Bognor and Dibdini liked Montin. It was, sort of, on a rich well-heeled tourist track, but it seemed not to care less and just gave a shrug, maybe said *pouf!* and carried on playing backgammon. Silverburger did not eat there. He preferred Cipriani and Harry's Dolci.

Both men were nearing retirement, which would come as a relief to alleged friends and foes alike. It was typical that Bognor worked in a department that most people would have thought could not possibly have anything to do with crime, while Dibdini operated from the one city in an endemically criminal society that had practically no crime at all and boasted a constant decline—a sort of criminal negative equity. These stratagems provided useful cover for these two least likely sleuths. Few people expected serious forensic detection from either Venice or the British Board of Trade. Such fools.

In another part of the city, tucked into a small palazzo on the other side of the Accademia Bridge between that forbidding gallery and the modern extravagances of Peggy Guggenheim's place, though a few meters nearer the Giudecca Canal, was a small exquisitely presented apartment out of whose full-length windows Sir Simon Bognor was staring absently as he thought of Guido Brunetti and Aurelio Zen and all the other overqualified mavericks who were connected with his favorite Italian city. The palazzo had been left to one of Bognor's friends and contemporaries from Apocrypha College, Oxford. The beneficiary, a genial, rather bright baronet, had not seen the palazzo coming and had been taken by surprise when a relative—distant, barely encountered, and not even recognizably English—had turned up her toes and left her home to her great-nephew by marriage on the grounds that he was the only one of her relations likely to appreciate the rotting old pile.

Rotting, it certainly was. In fact, had it not been for the battling baronet, the ancient house would have toppled head-long into the canal. Instead, he shored it up, bribed, cajoled, mixed cement with his bare hands, encouraged a dutiful wife to choose candelabra and carpets, fought and smiled and emerged, exhausted by his efforts but triumphant and the possessor of a magnificent mansion, parts of which he altruistically leased or lent to his friends and relations, depending on their means and their needs.

The Bognors were old friends and not particularly well-off. Consequently, they had the apartment for a song. Not even a dance.

Bognor stared out of the window and sighed. Venice tended to make him sad. It always had. Most cities were vibrant, traffic-clogged, teeming places with an obvious present and future; others, such as Pompeii or the possibly fictitious city of Lyonesse below the sea, were ruins. Venice, however, was a patient in the last stages of a terminal disease. You could argue that she was in remission, might even continue more or less serenely for a while yet, but she was obviously doomed and already, despite such deceptive evidences of contemporary living as the much publicized Questura, which acted as headquarters to the police force, she was dying. Bognor was as alive to the old girl's beauty as anyone, but he recognized the horrid truth, which was that she was in the last stages of her existence.

No wonder the place made him sad.

But, and it was a big and significant *but*, she was a wonderful old thing. Bone structure, breeding, you could call it whatever you wanted, but La Serenissima had a quality that was unique. He loved her and always would even if she sank beneath the "drill" philosophy that had found such an eerie expression in the American presidential election of 2008. Venice could have been saved, but the world was not the place in which to perform such an operation. The world was about money and profit and economics. Venice was concerned with matters ethereal, and there was no fusion between the two points of view.

Bognor sighed and tied a desultory knot in his Apocrypha tie. He remained a jacket-and-collar sort of person with a striped signifier discreetly threaded at the neck. God knew why he bothered. Upbringing, background—yes; oh, and deception.

Most people who wore striped-club or old-boy ties came from a striped-club, old-boy-tie background with all the baggage that was implied by such impedimenta. This didn't apply to Simon. He was entitled to the tie and the background was his, but if you judged him by this carapace, you would be making a mistake. It was a mistake frequently made, but it was a mistake nonetheless. He wasn't what he seemed.

Lunch at Montin with Dibdini. It would be like old times. Just the two of them. They had been lunching together at La Locanda Montin, hidden away behind its deliberately unobtrusive lantern, for longer than either man cared to admit. Both of them had become creatures of habit, which was something that seemed to Bognor to be a necessary concomitant of age. It was often suggested that one tended to be more Conservative as one got older, but the capital *C* was an irrelevance. It only counted insofar as it was a consequence of the lowercase article. The tendency not to tinker with anything if it worked, however imperfectly, was one that had become more pronounced as Bognor aged. So, of course, was the sense of having seen everything before. That was a product of years. Obviously. The longer one spent on Earth, the more chance one had of enduring repetition. This was true of big things and small. One day, England would win the Football World Cup. One day, World War III would break out. These were articles of Bognor's belief.

So was the inevitability of Venice's final demise. To think otherwise was to be a contemporary Canute. The sea would triumph just as the sea always did, and the great city would eventually sink beneath the waves, sooner rather than later if global warming was all it was cracked up to be. If he were a betting man, he would have checked the relative odds for the islands of the Venetian lagoon and Maldives. Smart money would be on Venice he reckoned, though the republic of Tuvalu might be worth a flutter. His affection for the city made this knowledge even more difficult to bear. Affection was too weak a word for what he felt, though. Like other Englishmen from Lord Byron and John Ruskin to John Julius Norwich, he felt passionately about Venice, even more so because he knew she was doomed. In that sense, she was more human than almost any other place he could think of.

"Penny for them," said Monica, his wife, who had come into the *piano nobile* without his noticing.

"Nothing," he lied absentmindedly.

"You don't do nothing," she said. "*Buzz, buzz!* Your thoughts may be bumping into one another and canceling one another out in all directions, but don't tell me there's a vacuum. I don't believe it. Michael. You were thinking about Michael."

"Maybe," he admitted. He gave up on the tie he'd been trying to knot, unraveled it with a jerk and started out all over again. "Maybe I *was* thinking about Michael. I haven't seen him for a year. Perhaps he's changed."

Lady Monica gave a subdued English version of what might otherwise have been a guffaw. The sound was derisive, disguised as a laugh but devoid of humor. It was also, if not quite ladylike, at least feminine. Discreet, therefore, but unmistakably scornful, not to say disbelieving. She did not believe much of what her husband said.

"Too late for him to change. Too late for any of us, as well you know."

She liked Venice, too, but not as much as her husband. The city was essentially feminine, which meant that a woman like Monica was alert to Venice's wiles, skeptical of her sophistry. She was also more of a fatalist than Simon. If it was written, then written it was, and no human agency could change it. If your name was on the bullet, then you had to bite on it. Nobody else had a chance. Monica was a realist and inclined to pessimism.

"He is him. You are you. *Ça, c'est tout,*" she said.

"Not necessarily," said Bognor. "Nothing is what it seems. It's like Conan Doyle said about the English countryside: happy, safe, smiling face, but actually she harbors more nefarious activity than the foulest urban sink or hellhole."

"Whereas Venice, which seems so sinister and saturnine, is actually safe as houses."

"You said it," Bognor agreed. "But then when you start believing that, life has an unpleasant habit of biting you in the bum and calling your double bluff."

"So," she said, taking over the tie-knotting herself with a shake of the head and a not very convincing display of uxorious exasperation, "Venice seems criminal, but actually isn't, but just when you become convinced that she's all gaudy ostentation, she spews up a corpse." She finished tying the knot in his gaudy striped tie and stepped back, smiling, to inspect her handiwork.

"In a manner of speaking," Bognor agreed, thanking her with a studiedly asexual peck on the cheek, "and Michael gives the impression of being a retired music master from a rather dim boarding preparatory school on the south coast of England."

"Precisely," she said, "and you think that tweedy exterior conceals a razor-sharp reality within. I, however, believe that the tweedy exterior conceals a tweedy interior. Just like you. It's part of the reason you're so attached to each other."

He made as if to cuff her. Her teasing was playful, but not entirely so; his response likewise. She was fond of him, very. But she was not convinced that he was any good at his job, much less that he deserved his knighthood. Feet of clay, which didn't mean to say she didn't love him. In fact, if he was as good as was sometimes alleged, she wouldn't have married him in the first place, and she certainly wouldn't have stayed with him for most of their natural adult lives.

"I'm running late," he said. "I'll see you in the Frari behind the altar around three fifteen." And he gave her another perfunctory kiss and left, heading for luncheon at La Locanda Montin.

3

"*Buon giorno*, Fred."

Bognor spoke Italian the way he spoke most foreign languages. He wished to communicate; he wished to appear friendly; he did not want to compromise his Englishness. Therefore, he adopted a Churchillian style with little or no concession to accent and a slight tendency to bombast. He liked being abroad; he liked foreigners; but he was true British through and through. He didn't believe in assimilation, inclining instead to difference. Nevertheless, he was extremely well disposed.

Hence "*Buon giorno,* Fred."

"*Buon giorno, signore,*" said Fred.

Fred was part of the scenery and always had been. He almost certainly wasn't called Fred, but that was what Bognor had originally christened him, and Michael had agreed, and Fred had entered into the joke if indeed it was a joke for it had become accepted and therefore natural. Fred had wispy white whiskers and wore a crumpled off-white linen jacket in which he appeared to sleep. His black tie was gray with age and gravy. Or *ragù*.

"Negroni?" asked Fred as Sir Simon entered the restaurant.

"*Mille grazie,*" said Bognor, knowing that Dibdini would already be sitting behind one. They always began with Negronis, named after the count who had invented them and who had died from a surfeit at a disgracefully tender age: Campari, gin, a slice of orange, a dash of soda. That was it. Maybe there was a little of some other kind of vermouth. He wasn't sure, but although the cocktails were lethal and should have rendered them incapable, they only made them mellow. Just the one. Which didn't prevent them from drinking wine with the meal and maybe having some sort of *digestivo* with the coffee. One did. One was abroad. With a friend. And Fred made them. His probably weren't the same as the one the count asked for when he wanted his *americano* strengthened that day in Florence; nor the one he bottled in the family distillery in Treviso where they played rugby, nor the one Orson Welles made popular when writing to that small town newspaper somewhere in Ohio, but what the hell, when in Venice. And Fred's Negronis or whatever they were, well . . .

"Hey, Michael. Wonderful. How good to see you. And you haven't changed a bit."

This was not true, but the expression and the hug and the double kiss that went with it, they were all part of the ritual, a small token of their friendship.

They stepped back, hands on opposite shoulders, surveyed each other head to toe, shook their heads, and sat down.

"Well," said Bognor, "who'da thunk it?"

It was always a pleasure to see each other, and they met often enough for change to be virtually imperceptible. Professional circumstance brought them together, but the bonds that bound them had nothing to do with work. They were the same sort of people: bright, indolent, depressed about the world in general but surprisingly happy with their own particular lot within this overall pretty ghastly scheme of things. Neither cared for authority, status, or people who liked to think they were in charge. Both were members of the awkward squad, but their appearance suggested a level of conformity and class that was deceptive and sometimes came as an unpleasant surprise to people who made assumptions.

They sat. Bognor's Negroni, aka Fred's Special, arrived. The silence was comfortable, and when Simon spoke, his question was comfortable as well.

"Busy?" he asked conversationally.

"It depends what you mean by busy," said the Italian. His English was perfect. He was blessed with perfect pitch and spoke several languages like a native. Even Swahili and Urdu.

"You know perfectly well what I mean." Bognor laughed,

enjoying the occasion. The sunlight was thin, almost frigid. They were the only two outside. You couldn't call it warm, especially for a Venetian. Maybe for an Englishman, though.

"We had a murder yesterday. A real one." No equivocation. No question of ambiguity: no question of was it or was it not natural causes or maybe an assisted suicide. This was a real murder. "A man was shot. In the back. One minute, he was alive and apparently fit and happy. The next minute, he was struck down."

"Hmmm." Bognor sipped his drink and was transported back through numerous similar occasions in the same place with the same man having much the same conversation. "You got the man who did it?"

"Man or woman." Michael smiled. "Can't be sure. We don't even have a witness."

"No witness?"

The Italian policeman studied his orange slice as if it were a potential witness and replied softly, "No witness. The driver of the boat was looking straight ahead. The deceased was the only passenger on board. The man from the hotel had turned to go indoors. We think he was killed soon after leaving, but it could have been almost anywhere along the Grand Canal. Everyone in the city was in disguise. It's Carnival."

"I'd noticed." Bognor spoke drily. Some people, like himself, were playing themselves, but just as many were playing the fool, unrecognizable in grotesque masks.

"We have the instrument of death."

"A bullet?"

"A bolt."

"From the blue." Bognor smiled, and Michael, who spoke perfect English even down to idiom, smiled with him.

"From a crossbow." He paused. "At least that's what my man says. He is speculative, of course. Doesn't want to be pinned down. Is as ambiguous as he dares."

"Crossbow," Bognor repeated fatuously.

Fred came to take their order, which was superfluous. It was always the same: *prosciutto e melone, fritto misto*, a carafe of the house white, a slice of *dolcelatte*, a double espresso, and maybe a glass of grappa. Always the same. Part of the ritual.

"Crossbows went out with the ark," said Bognor. "And always a distinctly foreign weapon. We went in for longbows. Agincourt and all that. Hearts of ash. Crossbows were for sissies and Europeans."

"Still quite lethal," said Dibdini. "Quiet to the point of virtual silence. And at this time of year as prevalent as a false nose or a tricorn hat."

"I suppose so," said Bognor. "And the stiff? Some sort of local? All dressed up and nowhere to go?"

"Not dressed up in the sense that I suspect you mean," said Dibdini. "A slightly lame vicuna overcoat, which might have seen better days. Savile Row tailored suit. Shirt from some shop in Jermyn Street. Underclothes and accessories likewise. Silly tie. Handmade. Silk. He was an American, I need hardly say."

"No," said Bognor. He supposed not.

Fred came with the *prosciutto e melone.* Also the carafe. Bognor snapped off a piece of grissino and chewed thoughtfully.

"Gay?"

"Seems to have batted and bowled," said Dibdini, "to judge from his address book. Professionals of every known sex plus some. One or two gifted and enthusiastic amateurs as well. Surprised he had time for anything else."

"Hmm." Bognor polished off his breadstick and looked thoughtfully at the *prosciutto e melone.* "What else? How did he make his money?"

"The money must have been considerable," said the Italian. "He was staying in a suite at the Danieli, ate in the most expensive places, and was using one of those new pink cards. Film."

"Porn?"

"Not as far as I can see. Pulp features. Things like *The Coffee Grinders.*"

"Not Silverburger?"

"Why? You know him?"

By way of answer, Bognor almost choked on his forkful of *prosciutto e melone.*

"Know him? Everyone knows Irving G. Silverburger," he said, hiccupping disbelievingly. "He's constantly in the gossip columns; he's always on TV. He's almost A-list. He's a celebrity—get him out of here."

"Someone just did," said Dibdini, managing his first mouthful of the antipasto better than the Englishman, "though I have to confess that he was not known in Italy. Most people had never heard of him. Myself included."

It was on the tip of his tongue to say something unpleasant about the third world, Italy, and Mr. Berlusconi, but Bognor thought better of it and simply allowed himself one of his all-purpose *I see*s which conveyed everything and nothing at the same time, depending on one's point of view.

"No, you don't," said his friend. "You think that because Italy had never heard of your Mr. Silverburger we are somehow a third-rate country and that I, in particular, being completely ignorant of this person, am also, in some sense, third rate. And I have to tell you that knowing nothing of this person is a badge of honor. He is typical of a world and of a culture that has happily passed us by. Our values are enduring and permanent and real. We spit on people such as your Silverburger."

"Speaks very highly of you," said Bognor, spearing another segment of *melone*, equanimity evidently restored.

Dibdini laughed. "No," he said, "and I am surely sorry that he is dead, but he was not a person of substance. Wealth, perhaps, and in your world, he may have enjoyed a passing notoriety. But your world is not our world."

It was on the tip of Bognor's tongue to say something disparaging, but he bit back what would probably have seemed like a cheap gibe and had more *prosciutto e melone*, a slug of dry yet aromatic wine, and tore a piece of crusty bread from the basket of rolls in front of him.

"I'm not going to get involved in a discussion of Irving G.

Silverburger's true value to society," he said, "nor are you. We might fall out about it. All I'm saying is that he was something of a household word in Britain. He may have been a four-letter word, but that's not the point. The point is that he was well known."

Fred removed the *prosciutto e melone* plates and brought the *fritto misto*—rings of squid, tiny fish, and scallops, all encased in light batter. The same the world over and available even in London, but tastier somehow here in Venice, even though Bognor sensed the lagoon was as full of human corpses as fish. Here, under a lemon sun, you could smell the Adriatic, and his friend wore a tweed jacket, which he would maintain was in some sense "classical English" but which only an Italian could wear. Better cut for a start. Bognor smiled in a general, nonspecific way. Silence here was golden. It was like the recipe for a perfect marriage in which one's spouse was the only person in the world who didn't have to speak during a long journey in the car. Monica was like that, or should be, the theory usually overwhelming the reality, if you saw what this meant.

The two friends squeezed lemons over their fish. The fruit had probably been on a local tree an hour or so earlier. Bognor liked the idea.

"So you've got a real live murder on your hands," he said, smiling.

"Indeed," said Dibdini. He smiled. "Good to have something to get your teeth into after all that tax evasion by old money. Correction, just *old* these days. The money's gone, even the family silver. That's the problem. They can't pay. Nothing left."

He grimaced.

"A real murder," said Bognor. "Now you see him, now you don't. Any publicity yet?"

"Not yet," said Dibdini. "We've kept the reptiles at bay. His passing is secret. Next of kin have yet to be informed."

"Did he have any family?" asked Bognor. "I never think of Silverburger being a family person, but he must have arrived in the usual way. I think of him as getting wherever he was without a trace, but there was presumably a mother and father."

"A sister," said the Italian, "somewhere out West. Father made automobiles in what used to be Detroit. Died ages ago. Mother, too. The sister lives in some small town in Middle America. Husband runs some sort of greasy spoon. Regular family. Not like Irving G."

"No," said Bognor, "I suppose not."

They ate their fish thoughtfully and more or less silently. They drank wine and water, tap, from tumblers.

"Cards at Christmas," said Dibdini, "regular as clockwork. That was all. No message. Just a line, always the same. 'Your little Sis.'" He shrugged. "Not so little if the photos are true. Obese."

"Photos?"

"The marvels of modern science. We checked the flat. My man sent them on the Net. JPEG or something. Magic but useful."

"I like magic," said Bognor, "when it's useful. Not when it isn't. Just gets in the way."

His friend grinned and speared squid.

"When it is useful," he said. "Even food has use, *sì*?" And he grinned, happy.

"*Sì*," said Bognor. He smiled back. Happy, too.

This was obviously going to be a case for Bognor. Like many of the best cases, it would not go through the normal channels. Bognor did not like the normal channels, mistrusted them and used unconventional methods wherever and whenever possible. This was obviously a classic case of nodding, winking, and committing as little as possible to paper. He preferred it that way. Always had. It made him enemies, but he liked that, too.

SIDBOT, the Special Investigations Department of the Board of Trade, was not what it seemed. In the sometimes-murky world of intelligence, counterintelligence, and espionage, very little was. Indeed, you could argue that every organization in that world was some sort of a front. Even the most obvious—MI6 and MI7—had bland exteriors that often concealed the lethal truth within.

SIDBOT was often overlooked, even by its peers. So-called "experts" tended to ignore the department within a department despite the fact that it was, in its own estimation at least, the ultimate lean machine and better connected and better at its job than any of its bigger and more cack-handed competitors. Parkinson had been, in his old-fashioned, unobtrusive way, one of the great operators. He was a classic back-of-the-room boy, unnoticeable, unnoticed, shadowy, and unknown. He lived a modest, unaffected suburban life, kept regular hours, inspired intense loyalty among friends and colleagues, including Bognor, and disdain among those who did not even think of themselves as rivals. If part of the game was not being noticed and not being reckoned, then people such as Parkinson, Bognor, and Contractor were past masters. Very few people even knew they existed. That was a huge strength, particularly in such a self-congratulatory world.

"He made *The Coffee Grinders*," said Bognor. "Produced, directed, wrote. Did everything but act. He left acting on screen to his employees. Off-screen he did lots."

Dibdini, his mouth full, nodded agreement. When he had swallowed, he said, "I'm afraid I didn't see it."

"Nor I," said Bognor.

"In Italian," said Dibdini, "it was called *Espresso*. The literal translation would have been *Macinacaffè*, which is not such a good title. *Espresso* is better."

"In English, the word refers to the machine and to the person who operates it. Sort of double entendre. That's not the case in Italian. An extra reason for *Espresso* being a better title. We have the word in English, too. In fact, it could have been a better title in England as well."

Dibdini looked noncommittal. "I understand it was a very poor movie," he said.

"Silverburger only made poor movies," said Bognor. "That was his stock-in-trade. People enjoyed them. It was what he was famous for and it made him a lot of money."

"Evidently." Michael looked pained.

"You have no idea who killed him?"

"None whatsoever," said his friend. "Could have been anyone. It was the middle of Carnival. A crossbow would have attracted no attention. It was simple. How do you say? 'Beautiful in its simplicity.'" He smiled with satisfaction at having got the phrase right.

"No leads?" said Bognor. "No ideas? Nothing?"

"Nothing whatsoever," Michael seemed to relish drawing a complete blank. "Our friend took a private water taxi from the Hotel Danieli to Marco Polo airport. Somewhere along the route, he was shot in the back by a bolt from a crossbow. It was Carnival time. The revelers wore masks. Many would have carried crossbows. A real-life assassin would have passed unnoticed. Did pass unnoticed."

"Maybe it was someone having target practice?"

The policeman spread his hands. "Possible."

"A joke?"

"Not in good taste, but also possible."

Michael speared the final piece of fish. "Everything is possible. All we know is that Mr. Silverburger was alive when he entered the boat and he was dead by the time he arrived at the airport. Beyond that, nothing. Nothing at all."

Fred cleared away their plates and brought the *dolce-latte*. The portions of blue-veined cheese looked stark and unadorned. Sometimes they had the *tiramisu* or the *tartuffo*. Latterly, elsewhere, they had tried the *affogato*—hot espresso, cold vanilla ice cream, and Amaretto. But not today. They always ate and drank the same. Today was the cheese. It was part of the ritual.

"A little grappa," suggested Michael, "with the coffee. To settle the stomach." The grappa had nothing to do with settling the stomach and they both knew it. They didn't care, but it was part of the ritual, so they ordered it. And it came with the coffee and another wispy smile from Fred, who was part of their game and knew it and enjoyed it as well.

"Your man Silverburger. He had a lot of enemies?" ventured Bognor.

"Not my man," said Michael. "God's perhaps. Or the devil's. And nobody liked him but nobody enough to kill."

"*Un crime passionnel*," said Bognor. "*Cherchez la femme.* Or in this case *le garçon*. Or something."

"Something possibly," said his friend. "He was insatiable and without discrimination. Anything, anyone that moved. He took a gondola down the canal soon after he arrived and invited the gondolier home. He came. Money changed hands. And bodily fluids." He laughed. "We have taken a statement. Maybe we should also speak to Benito's mother. And Benito's Doberman. The family goat?"

He drank coffee and smiled.

"You're incorrigible," said Bognor.

This was not a word in the Italian's English vocabulary, but he caught its gist and smiled.

Bognor smiled back. "On this trip, then, a gondolier called Benito? Anyone else?"

"He was seeking finance for his new movie. In English, I

think it was to be called *The Lemon Peelers*. In Italian, *Limoncello*. That would make both the English and Italian movies sequels, if you follow me. *Coffee Grinders*, *Lemon Peelers*; *Espresso*, *Limoncello*."

Michael smiled. Like so many Italians, he took pleasure in language, enjoying the noise, letting words and syllables luxuriate in his mouth, before escaping in an exhalation of onomatopoeia. Bognor enjoyed the sound of words, too, but had an almost Germanic interest in meaning. He viewed language primarily as a means of communication, not of entertainment. He valued precision, whereas Dibdini did not like meaning to interfere with a mellifluous sound. Like a journalist who did not allow the truth to interfere with a good story.

"You want me to be involved and yet not involved," said Bognor, returning to basics. His *moutons*, as the French would insist.

Dibdini said nothing but looked conspiratorial and acquiescent. This was how the two men liked to do business, with as much under the table as up front. It had become a trademark of SIDBOT so that newcomers to the corridors of power would sometimes ask one another, "What exactly does SIDBOT do?" and receiving no satisfactory answer would pass on. Bognor's attitude was that SIDBOT dealt in shadows, illusions, and poker. If they reflected that and played a real-life game of grandmother's footsteps and 'now you see me, now you don't,' then that meant the organization was only behaving in character.

"*Spremiagrumi*," said Fred, who was hovering around as always on the thin pretext of something to do with the coffee and/or grappa. He would have made a good spy; maybe was one.

"That's a juicer not a zester," said Bognor, not fazed and not changing rhythm nor breaking sweat. He accepted Fred and his perfect right to take part in their discussion.

Fred, for his part, didn't accept that what he had done was eavesdropping let alone what Bognor was brought up to call 'picking up fag ends.' He was an equal partner. Just because he was a waiter didn't mean that he was some kind of inferior. He had just as much right to express a view as either of the two. Just because they had paid and he was getting paid. It was different in England. Waiters were by definition inferior to those upon whom they waited. Elsewhere, it was not the same, and there were even countries mainly in the gastro-nomically developed world where the reverse was true. Jack was not only as good as his master; he was better.

Neither Bognor nor Dibdini was stupid or snobbish enough to ignore Fred's thoughts. They were not gullible enough to believe everything he said, but they listened. Unusual, but both men prided themselves on their open minds.

"So you want me to have a look at Silverburger's life in London."

"My understanding is that he spent much of his life in your country. He had several dwellings around the world, but he seems to have been based in London. He was what I believe you call a 'non-dom.' His films were made in studios in the United Kingdom. The locations were wherever he could broker a deal."

"Where he could do something on the cheap?"

"He did not like to spend money," said Dibdini, "except possibly on himself. But even then he preferred to have someone else paying the money."

"Who were his benefactors?"

"That is what I am asking you," said Dibdini. "We know that he was seeking finance here in Venice, but we know very little about his activities in the United Kingdom. You, my old friend, are expert in such matters. Even if you do not know, you can discover."

Michael was surprisingly ham-fisted when it came to flattery.

Bognor smiled and sipped first coffee and then grappa.

"So you do the Italian end, and I do the English. And we compare notes on a regular basis. Should we develop a watertight case, then it's your baby."

"The murder was committed here in Venice, so it's my problem," he said. He raised a glass. "Cheers!" he said. "So we have a deal? And how is Monica? Or should I say Lady Bognor? She is with you? Will you be going to Torcello? Is there a concert? An exhibition? What brings you here?"

Bognor sighed. "This," he said. "That. You. No, she'll always be Monica to the two of us. And Signora Dibdini? Laura?"

"Laura is fine," said Dibdini.

The wives did not get on; nor the wives and their husbands' foreign counterpart. Pity. It didn't interfere with the relationship between the two men, and it didn't impinge, either. They were both uxorious in their different ways and yet also very masculine in an old-fashioned way. There was something of the bachelor about both—a whiff of tweed and leather and eau de cologne. They liked books and libraries and the sort of food one associates with the better boarding schools and gentleman's clubs: savories, claret, oysters, game. Their wives were much more emancipated and progressive. To those who didn't know both, Bognor and Dibdini might have seemed old-fashioned. Very few people began to understand what they were doing with Monica and with Laura. Yet their women were vital, and if you didn't understand that and if you didn't get the relationship and its importance, then you would always find them unfathomable. Which most people did.

"Doesn't seem a very nice man," said Bognor, stating the obvious.

"But successful," said Dibdini. "Contemporary society seems to like that kind of person. Life today is little other than one Silverburger after another."

This, too, was a statement of the obvious.

"He won't be missed," said Bognor.

"Maybe not," said Dibdini, "but he was alive, and now he is dead. And this was not natural. Not what was meant. Someone has interfered with the natural course of events. A religious person would say that the murderer got in the way of God."

"Yes." Bognor knew that. Neither man was religious, but they had respect for those who were. They did not believe in God, but part of each of them wished that they did and had affinity for those who had that belief. Aside from which, much of their jobs consisted of resisting an interference with which they basically agreed. Most of those who were murdered got what they deserved and even what they were asking for. This, however, was something which neither the special investigator nor the superior Italian policeman realized until after they had entered their profession. By then, it was too late.

"We're better off without him."

Dibdini raised his glass and nodded.

"The world, too," continued Bognor.

They agreed about that, too.

"We still have a job to do," said Dibdini.

"You, in this case."

"Not now," said Dibdini. "We are agreed. The job is ours. We may not like it. But it is ours. It is shared."

Bognor thought about this. Then it was his turn to raise his glass and to nod. He said nothing, but they understood each other.

4

Irving G. Silverburger was not a nice man, dead or alive.

This was a hazard of Bognor's job. He had discovered over the years that it was more than possible to establish a rapport with murderers, but that those they killed were often unpleasant. You could even argue that they had it coming to them. Death, that was. It came to everyone sooner or later, a cliché that Bognor kept at the forefront of his mind most of the time and preferred to describe as a truism. Bognor's job was to try to minimize the artificially induced early arrival of this universal fact and to punish those responsible. He was not a great believer in rehabilitation and, though not religious, tended to subscribe to the doctrine of original sin. It should also be conceded that murder cases, though high profile and on the whole enjoyable, were not the stuff of his life, which had much more to do with pieces of paper, customs, and excise, and useless clutter of daily life.

He and Lady B. spent a happy few days in La Serenissima and came home sated with dubious seafood, painting, music, and the novels of Salley Vickers. Both had a good time, and it wasn't until his return to the office that Bognor's thoughts turned to the dead Mr. Silverburger. Contractor's report was on his desk. At the top. Mandatory reading.

Reading carefully took him the best part of half an hour. He read the print, of course. But also—as required and, as he always did—he read between the lines as well. At the end of it, he liked the late Mr. Silverburger even less than at the outset. If such a thing were possible, which seemed unlikely.

He buzzed for Contractor, who came running, though not breathless. Bognor noted the alacrity and the youth and fitness and came to his point.

"Nasty piece of work."

"You could say that, Boss."

"I just did."

"Right. I agree. Should have been able to get to the airport without a crossbow bolt between the shoulder blades, though."

"True." It was his point entirely. Just because Silverburger was a waste of space didn't mean that you had to shoot him. If that were the case and SIDBOT had a license to kill, there would be no one left on the planet.

"Do you think there was anyone in London who might have killed him?"

"Difficult to say, Boss," said Contractor, hedging his bets like the good civil servant he was. It was the correct response, but unhelpful. Bognor knew better than to expect anything else to such a question.

He thought of asking if Contractor thought the murderer lived in London but thought better of it.

"Was he sleeping with Ingrid Vincent?" he asked instead.

It was obviously on the tip of his subordinate's tongue to come up with something that was open to any one of a number of different interpretations, but Contractor clearly thought two ambiguities in a row was too much.

"Probably," he said. "Silverburger slept with anything that moved, and Miss Vincent distributed her favors to anyone she thought might help her. If she thought Silverburger would get her work, she'd have sex with him. The casting couch. It's an old tradition in celluloid circles."

"Grandmother," said Bognor.

This was a private code that basically meant don't teach your grandmother to suck eggs; meaning in plain English that Contractor should not tell his boss things that he knew perfectly well already, especially when these had to do with common practice. Bognor knew that aspiring film stars were traditionally supposed to sleep with producers of movies in which they coveted work. He had also heard the ancient story about the dumb blonde who slept with the writer by mistake. He suspected that Silverburger was a past master of the casting-couch ploy.

"So is Ingrid a suspect?" he asked.

"Lousy actress. Loose morals. Big boobs. I'd say yes, but I have no evidence."

"That'll do for now. Anyone else?"

"Ingrid was in *The Coffee Grinders*," said Contractor, "which means that she had form. In a manner of speaking. All she had to do was flaunt her breasts and pout. Both of which came naturally."

"Figures," said Bognor. "And to a lesser degree, every winnable starlet in London. What about Trevor?"

"Helps out at tea parties," said Contractor. "In other words, gay as all get-out. Looks after the flat that is one of those 1920s mansion jobs off Kensington High Street. I just have a feeling in my bones that there's no sex involved and that it really is a professional arrangement. Don't ask me how or why. But that's my feeling."

"So you rule him out?"

Contractor considered. "I wouldn't rule him out, but I wouldn't have him on my A-list, either. Certainly not near the top. Don't ask me why; it's just a hunch."

Contractor's hunches might not stand up in court, but they were usually right. Which is why Bognor was inclined to work on them.

"But you do have a feeling about the accountant? The financial adviser, that is."

"Bromley man," said Contractor. "Yes. Don't ask me why. He doesn't fit into any pattern. Rather the reverse. I just don't feel happy about him."

"In what sense?"

"He's just too obviously innocent," Contractor said perversely. "Married. Lives in Bromley. Rotarian. Thousands like him. Regular little pooter—salt of the earth and all that. *Telegraph* reader."

"So we have a gay factotum who sounds deeply suspicious, but who you maintain is innocent; and an innocent seeming Bromley man, who you perversely consider high on the list of potential perpetrators?"

"If you put it like that, then I suppose so, yes."

"Good God, man! Have you no respect for the rules of evidence?" shouted his boss. Then he calmed down. "That's what I should be asking," he explained, "but I know you too well. And I trust your instinct. Anyone else?"

"Loads," said Contractor, "but that's my short list. In a manner of speaking. Up to a point. Ingrid is obvious. You have to include Trevor even if only because he has to be on everyone else's list. Eric has to be in because he's on mine even if he doesn't feature elsewhere."

"Eric Swanley?"

"You've read my report," said Contractor. "Good."

"What about the other suspects?"

"Everyone hated Silverburger. It went with his territory. But those are the only people worth considering. There are plenty of other candidates who will be glad he's gone, but no one who would have sent him there. If you get what I mean."

"Such as?"

Contractor smiled. "Oh," he said, "the postman; the Polish

couple who ran the deli; the neighbors, especially the ampu-
tee next door on the left; the vicar; the woman from Citizen's
Advice; the lollipop people from outside the school; the man
in the blue overalls who spent so much time under the car."
He paused. "I could go on."

"I'd rather you didn't," said Bognor. "Ingrid Vincent,
Trevor, and Eric Swanley. Does Trevor have a second name?"

"Not so as you'd notice," said Contractor, "but I can
find out. Ingrid Vincent is Romanian. Ingrid is sort of half
right; only it's something like Inge. And her second name is
Pupescu. If my name was Inge Pupescu, I'd change it. She
took Vincent because her first British boyfriend was the
Oxford University hooker."

"And he was a member?"

"Right." Contractor was impressed but tried not to show it.

"And don't tell me Eric Swanley isn't his real name."

"He was christened Eric all right, but his name should be
Braun. His parents came from Germany. Leipzig, I think.
Swanley was the nearest appropriate place to Bromley so
they called themselves that."

"As one would."

"Well," said Contractor, "why not? Better than Braun.
Particularly spelled that way. *Wie geht es, braun Kauw?*"

"Cow in German is '*Kuh*.'"

"I know that," Contractor said testily. "Unless it's part of a
meal in which case it's probably *Rindfleisch*."

"Or steak," said Bognor. "Medium-rare-steak-*mit*-chips-
und-horseradish and whatever the German for mustard is."

"*Senf,*" said Contractor. "*Französicher Senf* or *Englischer Senf* but, for some reason, never *Kraut Senf.* Odd that. You'd think the Germans would be rather good at mustard."

"In any event," said Bognor, "I'm not the least bit surprised that old man Braun changed the family name to Swanley. Was he an accountant, too?"

"Worked in the docks," said Contractor. "Snuffed out by a Doodlebug toward the end of the war. Some sort of office job. Paper shuffler. Nothing as glorified as accountancy, but it probably had to do with figures."

Bognor had a mental picture of the sad refugee Braun who had become Swanley and fathered Eric before Braun senior was done in by a doodlebug minding other people's business in the docks.

"Sad," he said.

"And now little Eric is working for a guy called Silverburger," said Contractor. "Makes you think, eh?"

"Doesn't pay to think too much," said Bognor. "Makes you depressed."

"You should know," said Contractor. He was being playful in a mindless way.

"So," said Bognor, "you think we should tell Italy that we've identified three potential suspects: Ingrid Vincent, née Pupescu; Trevor; and Eric Swanley, né Braun."

"Why not?" Contractor asked rhetorically.

Bognor picked up a pencil from the desktop and began to tap it ruminatively about the palm of his left hand.

At length, he said, "Because there are countless, literally

countless, people in the city who would like to have shot Irving Silverburger and killed him. They believed that the world would be a better place without him, and I'm bound to say that they had a point."

He paused.

"We, on the other hand, have whittled down the list of suspects to just three. When I say *whittled*, I use the word advisedly, for the whittling has been done as it were by the seat of one's pants. All three had good reason for wishing the deceased dead. On the other hand, you could argue that they also had good reason for keeping him alive. He paid, or was in a position to pay, their grocery bills, their mortgages. They owed their livelihoods to him. And yet he must have been excessively tiresome to have around and especially to be beholden to."

He continued to hit his hand rhythmically with the pencil, starting to hum as he did so. For no particular reason, the tune he hummed was the Italian national anthem, that interminable piece of sub-Verdi that suddenly took on a new lease of life just as one was resuming one's seat. It was the tune they played whenever a Ferrari won a Grand Prix. Which was often. Or before a rugby union international, which Italy lost just as often, despite large numbers of Australians with hitherto unsuspected Italian grandmothers.

"Originally written in 1847. Words by a twenty-year-old poet named Goffredo Mameli and set to music by Michele Novaro. It was adopted as the national anthem just over a century later. They used to play the march of the Royal House of Savoy before that. Il Duce had a lot to answer for."

"Not many people know that," said Bognor, deriding his subordinate's apparently bottomless fund of useless information. "But I don't care. I like it."

"Me, too. Bit heavy on *Italia*, but still a good tune."

"So you're going with the three suspects?"

"If you insist," said Contractor. "But my hunch is that none of them could be bothered to travel to Venice, acquire a crossbow, and shoot Silverburger in the back. They could just as well have done it here. Slit his wrists or given him arsenic."

"Good way to kill," his boss said thoughtfully. "I mean if one had to go prematurely, it's quite a smart way of shuffling off. Wouldn't have known anything about it. Instantaneous. One minute, you're in a sleek motorboat heading down the Grand Canal; the next, *pouf!* you're God knows where."

"His departure had a lot more style than anything else he did," conceded Contractor. "Better than anything in his films."

"Maybe," said Bognor. "I wonder if Signora Pupescu would agree. Or Trevor. Or Mr. Braun."

"Does your friend have good suspects?" asked Contractor. "I bet it was an Italian job. Brits don't have that sort of bravura."

Bognor demurred, "We're talking about a German, a Romanian, and Trevor. I'm assuming Trevor is British."

"Sorry," said Contractor. "Latvian. A Balt anyway. And Trevor isn't his real name, either."

"No," said Bognor, "of course not. So we have a German, a Romanian, and a Latvian. In Venice with a crossbow. And the deceased was an American national, but with a name like Irving G. Silverburger you're not, I hope, going to pretend that he was a Native American."

"No Navajo he," agreed Contractor. He was apparently on the verge of thinking better of this but sensibly decided against it and shut up.

"Get me Venice," said his boss.

5

"Michael," said Bognor, not only speaking into what appeared to be thin air but, courtesy of something called Skype, which he didn't understand but seemed to work and to cost nothing, addressing a picture of his old friend on a screen in front of him. Flat. Thin. State-of-the-art. Courtesy of Contractor.

"Simon," Dibdini was looking a little pale, puffy, almost peaky. Too much grappa and improbably small and chemically damaged fish from the Adriatic. Bognor knew he really must give up cheroots but had seldom felt better. Positively bounding with bonhomie and good health.

"The Silverburger case," said Bognor, coming straight to

the point. "We've whittled down the field and come up with three possible suspects."

Michael nodded but said nothing.

"His live-in factotum, a young Latvian called Trevor; his accountant, Eric Swanley, originally Braun; and Ingrid Vincent, née Pupescu, a not-as-pulchritudinous film actress as she would like."

Bognor was mildly irritated with this lapse, lulled into a sense of complicity by the tweed. Michael didn't do pulchritudinous.

"No English?" complained the Italian.

"We don't do English any longer," said Bognor, "though that sounds like a BNP line. Which I am definitely not."

"I would like to have one English villain," complained Michael. "Silverburger, also. I am sure he always had an English villain in his pictures. An odious person from what you still think of as the top drawer, stroking his waxy mustaches and talking through his nose."

"Down his nose, not through his nose," said Bognor. "No chin and he would probably not have been to Eton. Chucked out of somewhere inferior for something grubby to do with lead off roofs or possibly some shopgirl from the town. Have you identified some good Italian criminals?"

His friend had the grace to laugh.

"Italy has the world's best criminals," he said. "Most come from the south and work in the United States. In the north, our criminals are not in the same league. Good but not really world class. We gave the world the Mafia, the Cosa Nostra, and respect, not to say respectability. It is one of our gifts to the world."

"Silverburger was some kind of Balt. At least his ancestors were," said Bognor. "But that proves nothing. Balts don't have the monopoly on crummy B-list movies any more than you have a monopoly on crime. The British do a good line in murder, and we have some top-whack hoodlums. The Krays were good."

"The Krays were average," said Michael, smiling. "Not in our league. The only area in which the British are world class when it comes to crime is in the cad. Your George Sanders is top of the class. A world leader."

"So what," inquired Bognor, "do you have when it comes to the Silverburger murder?"

"First," said Dibdini, splaying out fingers and seeming to count, "there is Benito, the sexy gondolier. I do not believe he is a killer, but he has to be on our list. Then there is Sophia, also a professional and one Mr. Silverburger acquired professionally. She was, is, some kind of Russian I believe. Many Russians come to Venice for professional sex. Then there are Gina and Bernardo, who were going to put money and talent into *Limoncello*, or *The Lemon Peelers*, whichever you prefer, and were the main reason for Mr. Silverburger coming to our city. Oh, and Father Carlo."

"Father Carlo?"

"*Sì*. Father Carlo is *very* interesting. Your friend Mr. Silverburger went to confession heard by Father Carlo in the Frari. Father Carlo is a Franciscan. Well, maybe. He has a reputation in the city. Little boys; little girls. He is extremely corrupt, very bad, but clever and very interesting. He enjoys whiskey, and Silverburger presented him with some Johnny Walker Blue Label, which is Father Carlo's favorite drink. He has Blue Label for breakfast, lunch, and tea, but he is never drunk. Tipsy maybe, but not drunk. He finds young people who have no money and no morals, so I have him on my list. He plays the fiddle. He gives lessons in music. He plays very well. Maybe he is Italian, but I am not sure. He is very difficult to touch because he has friends in what you refer to as high places. Cultivated and corrupt. A very bad man indeed. I would like to have him put away, but it is exceedingly difficult. Impossible to pin anything on him. He is slippery as a serpent."

"Eel," said Bognor.

"What?" asked Michael. "I said serpent. Snake, perhaps. He is a snake that likes to hide in the long grass; his bite is fatal; his taste is catholic but depraved. He and your friend Silverburger became very close very fast. As you would say, they hit it off."

"He was not my friend," said Bognor. "Eel. Slippery as an eel. Old English saying."

"Not snake?"

"Not snake," said Bognor. "Not in colloquial English. Eel. Father Carlo is slippery as an eel. He is Calabrian. Not one of us."

"From Reggio," confirmed Dibdini. "His father had a shop. Father Carlo is expert in films."

"So," said Bognor, "you have Benito, the gondolier; Sophia, the Russian tart; Gina and Bernardo, the film financier and his would-be actress wife; and Father Carlo, the Machiavellian priest. Got anywhere with any of them?"

Dibdini looked like everybody's picture of frustration. The correct answer was nowhere, but that wasn't for want of trying, nor for lack of corroborative evidence. The crucial fact, however, was that one needed to prove that one of the suspects had gone out in the middle of Carnival armed with a crossbow, which he—or she—had used to kill Mr. Silverburger as he presented a broad-backed target in the back of the water taxi. This was difficult for there were no witnesses and, short of a crossbow turning up at the home of one of the suspects, no evidence. Even a useless murderer would surely have disposed of the weapon.

"No," he finally managed. He had tried. God knows he had tried, but he had failed.

"Gina and Bernardo," said Bognor. "Gina and Bernardo who?"

"Gina and Bernardo Ponti," said Dibdini. "They are well known here."

"Not here," said Bognor. "World famous in Venice. Maybe in Italy. Unknown here. They obviously don't travel."

"But, yes. They are often in England. Southampton. Northampton. Easthampton. Westhampton. Hampton Wick. Hampton Court. Something to do with Hampton. They have an apartment in the country. Bernardo likes to be the English gentleman. Gina is the English lady."

"Sounds like Northamptonshire," he said. "Cut-price Cotswolds. You can pick up a flat in a listed pile for a song. No dance needed. And the locals don't know any better. They probably think Bernardo is some sort of Italian aristo; Gina a contessa. Silverburger would have cut quite a dash there. Not many in Northants have ever been to Riga. There was a Balt car company there for a while. Russian-German. Went belly-up in the early twenties."

"Silverburger had been with Gina and Bernardo in the English countryside. With Trevor. His catamite."

"He wasn't his catamite," Bognor said stiffly. "He was his gentleman's gentleman. A sort of butler."

"Another Balt."

"Trevor was Latvian," said Bognor, as if that were different.

"Most Balts are Lithuanians or Latvians," said Dibdini, as if he had known this forever along with every schoolboy. He had actually only known about it since delving into Silverburger's ancestry. "The point is that the Pontis were impressed by the film business and they were impressed by the English. So when the two came together as they did with Silverburger then they were doubly impressed."

"But Silverburger made rubbish films," said Bognor, "and he wasn't English."

"The Pontis didn't know that. As far as they were concerned, he was both. He took them around the Saint James's district of London. He took them to the film studios at Ealing and at Pinewood. Everywhere he went, he seemed to be accepted. The English are like that. They remain polite, though perhaps it is some sort of fear. Perhaps they are frightened of foreigners, of those who are, as you say, all mouth and no trousers. They are scared of those who boast because they would like to be the same. Instead, they are understated. They never blow trumpets, never brag. Sometimes they never seem to know who they really are, even to themselves."

"So," said Bognor, "you're telling me that the Pontis invited Silverburger to their pad in Northants because they thought he was an English gentleman and because they assumed he was Cecil B. DeMille. Interesting combination."

Dibdini said he supposed so and that the corollary was that when in Venice they paraded him around town as their English friend, a brilliant filmmaker, friend of everyone who was anyone, and so on. In return, Silverburger thought he might touch Bernardo for some of the millions that he didn't really have. The price of the investment was an involvement in the new project for Gina on account of the looks and the talent in which she alone believed. The whole affair was the doomed building of one artifice on top of another. It was bound to end in failure and recrimination based on discovery. But murder? That was something else.

"Maybe," agreed Bognor, "but the problem is that this is in some ways the perfect crime. Let's say that the Pontis, or one of them, were the killer; that the motive was revenge, even that they benefited in some way. Then how can you prove it? You need witnesses; you need the crossbow. Even an Italian court needs evidence."

"Italian courts," said Dibdini, "were dealing in evidence when your people were still grappling with Magna Carta and thinking that the jury system was democratic and fair."

They often argued about juries, adversarial systems, Roman law, and suchlike. The disagreements were profound, extreme, and unresolved.

"I don't like Gina and Bernardo," said Dibdini.

"Nor do I," said Bognor, "but that doesn't make them murderers. I don't like the idea of Silverburger, and the odds are that he was killed by someone nice for all the right reasons. That doesn't make the murder right. Sorry. Maybe it should but justice isn't like that. It's not about punishing the nasty for doing something in character to victims we like. More often the reverse. Our job is still to establish the truth."

"Sometimes," said Dibdini, "I do not care for the truth."

"No," said Bognor, "but that doesn't prevent it being the truth. We don't like the Pontis. We rather hope that they are the murderers, but we look unlikely to be able to prove it. What about Father Carlo?"

"Ah, Father Carlo."

Silence.

"I rather like the idea of Father Carlo," said Bognor. "He is so repulsive, I end up being quite fond of him. He comes out the other side if you know what I mean."

"I know what you mean," said Dibdini, "and I have the

beginnings of a case against him. His hobby was medieval weaponry and, in particular, the crossbow."

Bognor laughed. "Good start," he said, "but a bit circumstantial. Just because Father Carlo was interested in the weapon that killed Irving G. doesn't make him a murderer."

"No," said his friend, "but it's a strange coincidence."

"Okay," said Bognor. "Was Silverburger really a Catholic?"

"If he was anything," said Dibdini. "Catholics believe in forgiveness. It's central. Silverburger believed in forgiveness. He believed in confession. Father Carlo can't tell us anything that passed between them in the Frari, but we know that Silverburger went to see him after he had slept with Sophia, the Russian prostitute, and after he had also had sex with Benito, the gondolier."

"So he was feeling guilty about them?"

"No," said Michael, "but he knew he had to confess. It is not the same. Father Carlo would have listened to what Silverburger had to say, and then he would have pursed his lips and made Silverburger say he was truly sorry, and he would have made him say some Hail Marys or something similar, and that would be it. Silverburger would leave the Frari with a clean sheet."

This didn't happen in the Church of England, even when one had lapsed.

"I don't understand Catholicism," he said.

"That's the point," said Dibdini. "You're not supposed to understand. It is literally beyond belief. Their rules are not our rules. The servant of the Lord preaches perpetual forgiveness because ultimately his master is the one who decides. He is the one who has power; he is the one who decides what is right and what is wrong."

"I see," said Bognor. Which is what he always said when he didn't.

6

The flat was comfortable, expensive—though it had been cheap when they first acquired it—and above shops in Marylebone High Street that had become quite a fashionable part of London by the early years of the twenty-first century. In a sense, it had caught up with them for when they had first bought it, many years earlier, it was what they could afford—no more and no less. It had always seemed a friendlier part of London than most of the city. There were fewer transients and it felt comfortable, a place full of the sort of shop and eating place where they remembered your name after just one or two visits.

London, meanwhile, had become arguably more glamorous, more vibrant and buzzy, but it had unquestionably become more dangerous. The homeless were everywhere. One felt hassled and threatened at every juncture. Smiling at strangers was a provocation; footsteps were almost certainly hostile, and there were muscle-bound bouncers in ever doorway. The higher the gloss, the greater the threat.

Marylebone had changed but less than other parts of town. It felt lived in, comfortable in the way that old clothes feel comfortable. There was a shabbiness, a down-at-heel gentility with which the Bognors felt at home. They recognized; they were recognized. When London was described as a set of interconnecting villages, they nodded in agreement. Elsewhere, they might have been, rightly, bewildered. Here, they felt, just as correctly, at home.

Monica was wearing a caftan. She always wore a similar garment when they were at home, relaxing and not expecting company. The shapeless bell-tent was as comfortable, homely, and frayed about the edges as the surroundings. She felt relaxed. Her husband in gray flannel bags, a shapeless cardigan, and slippers likewise. In their sort of England, it was bad form to drop in unannounced and the only probable phone calls would be from the subcontinent and have to do with debt or double-glazing. They would therefore ignore the telephone bell just as they would ignore any ring from the front door. Either would be an unwelcome intrusion.

"Well?" she asked.

"How do you mean?" It was a boiled-egg-and-toast sort of an evening and none the worse for that.

"Did you talk to Michael? About Mr. Silverburger?"

"Oh, that," he replied. "Yes. He sent his love."

"But what did he say?

The Bognors shared everything. Including secrets. Especially secrets.

"The Pontis have a place in Northamptonshire. Correction: They rent a place in Northamptonshire. Pass themselves off as local gentry."

"With any success?"

"Not a lot." He thought of the unchanging snobbery of the English countryside. "Eyeties don't go down a bomb with the Northants's smart set."

"I didn't think Northants had a smart set."

His wife had a good ear, nose, and throat for social pretension, being as near as dammit the real thing and close enough anyway to be able to tell the difference. If she wasn't related to the Northants's smart set, she had been to school with it. Or played tennis. Whatever, she looked down on it just as she looked down on practically everything and everyone.

"What about our suspects?" They were both drinking their evening whiskey, which was sort of medicinal and went with boiled eggs and toast. "Surely, we have a list as good as Dibdini's. I'd hate to think we were being beaten by the Italians at anything more serious than the Eurovision song contest."

"Not dissimilar." They always had a scotch if they were alone in the evening. Bell's, Teacher's, or the Famous Grouse, depending on what was on offer at Tesco. Regular as clockwork at about six thirty. He wondered vaguely if that made him an alcoholic or merely a creature of habit. Also if it mattered. Probably not. "One starlet who can't act; one servant figure from Latvia or thereabouts; and an accountant who was originally some sort of Kraut. Motives are: ambition crossed with sex, that's Ingrid, aka Inge; money and sex, that's Trevor the Balt, servitor; and money, that's Eric, who's the money man from Deutschland. I don't think sex comes into the game with Eric, so if he's the guilty party, it will be to do with expenses or VAT or petty cash fiddling. I somehow doubt it's huge amounts, but I could be wrong."

"And Silverburger wasn't a Member of Parliament," said Monica, "or a Tory benefactor who took advantage of non-dom status. A Labour Party donor who was double-crossing Unite. A Liberal who danced too vigorous a two-step with that nice Mr. Cable."

"I imagine Eric always votes Conservative because it's a mark of respectability," said Bognor, "but I'd be surprised if he were political enough to kill for his beliefs."

"Or courageous," said Monica. "Eric sounds quintessentially cowardly."

"Maybe," said her husband, "but I wouldn't be too certain. Money does odd things to the most ordinary-seeming people. Greed is a great motivator. Poverty is an excuse for all manners of excess. Swanley saw a lot of the stuff but never had very much himself. That transforms some people."

"I'd still prefer your Romanian starlet. Or even the poofter from Riga."

"We know nothing about his sexual proclivities," Bognor said pompously. And was rewarded with a pout of skepticism. She didn't believe him, couldn't believe he could be so naive.

"A Balt who calls himself Trevor. Come on." She smiled. "No straight Balt would call himself Trevor."

"And how many accountants do you know who would solemnly go to Venice to murder a client with a crossbow?"

Monica felt she had known one or two exotic accountants in her time, and yet the profession had a dull reputation. Good cover, she always felt. No one would ever expect the accountant of having done it.

"Well," she said, "just because they're accountants doesn't mean . . ."

"I'll see the Swanleys," said Bognor. "And I'll do so with an entirely open mind. I just don't happen to think he's our man."

"Whereas Trevor could be."

"Trevor," said Sir Simon, with all the authority of one who had never met him, "is single, foreign, and no better than he should be. He might easily hop over to Venice, mingle with the crowd, shoot the boss, and go home again. Jolly cheap on easyJet and perfectly convenient. Now you see me; now you don't."

"It's no easier for a single Latvian than for a married accountant," she protested.

"There," he said triumphantly. "Just the words suggest everything. The one is a plausible killer, and the other isn't. It's as simple as that."

"You've been exposed to too much Agatha Christie. You believe in Hercule Poirot and his little gray cells."

Bognor flushed. There was a smidgen of truth in this. He enjoyed the novels of the dame, but he was also scrupulous in distinguishing between fact and fiction, real life and the world according to Christie.

"I enjoy the Belgian and his little gray cells, but that isn't the same as believing in them."

"Not entirely from where I stand," she said. This was unfair and she knew it. "What I'm saying," she said, stepping back in an effort to seem slightly less partisan herself, "is that you're biased in favor of accountants against Latvians."

Simon decided to ignore this. She was being silly. He could not afford bias. Not in his job. It was essential to begin with a clean slate, and even if he had prejudices, it was important to distinguish between his personal views and his professional behavior. He tended to believe, along with P. D. James, that murder was essentially a working-class business, even if it became more interesting in middle-class hands. In this sense, he was classist. Yet he never allowed such beliefs to interfere with the way in which he conducted a case. Life had a way of surprising even him.

"Everyone gets questioned," he said. "You know that. And in exactly the same way. And everyone in my investigations is guilty until proved innocent. That's the way with investigators. We're the exact opposite of judges and juries. We have nasty suspicious minds. We believe the worst of everybody."

"Oh," said Monica. "Nothing nastier than a High Court judge. Prurient cross-dressers, the lot of them."

She was winding him up. This was something she often did when she was losing an argument.

"I know," he conceded. "There's a routine. It doesn't change a lot. What makes life interesting is the people we investigate, not the way we do it. That doesn't change. The people are always different though. That's what makes the job so fascinating."

"So you're a dull stick and all around you is ever-changing interest. Some of your best friends are murderers."

There was some truth in this, although privately Bognor thought he was quite interesting and rather unorthodox, preferring not to plod along with the rule book but to extemporize, sometimes with some brilliance and panache. Colleagues seemed not, on the whole, to notice and to be disparaging when they did. He cared about this, but tried to keep quiet about it.

"I'm always telling you that the essence of successful detective work is a constancy when faced with ingenuity and originality. That's almost the only fixed point in our line of work. Everything else is always different; that's why it is vital that I remain the same."

"Says you." She was smiling.

"I'm sorry if you think that's boring," he said, pretending to be affronted.

"I didn't say you were boring. Far from it. I only hinted that your approach to the job might be, well, shall we just say, blinkered."

He did not respond to this but said instead, "The only possible source of DNA was the bolt. No traces of anything. Whoever fired it was obviously wearing gloves. They knew what they were doing."

"Hired assassin?"

"Possible," he said. "It was Italy, after all. My gut tells me that it wasn't. I'm not used to it. It's not the way we do things here."

"But as you said this was abroad."

"And I said it was possible. I just believe that the killer was the person who wanted Silverburger dead. Don't ask me why. I just believe it."

"Difficult shot?"

"Not really. Silverburger was standing with his back to the bowman. To judge from the way the bolt penetrated, it was fired at close range. I assume whoever pulled the trigger had been practicing, so they knew what they were doing."

"So it could have been one of ours?"

Sir Simon thought for a moment.

"In theory, yes," he said. "If they happened to be in Venice. That's the main stumbling block."

"But easily ascertained."

"Easily ascertained, yes."

They both stared moodily into their emptying glasses.

"He was a ghastly man, Silverburger," he said eventually.

"So they say," agreed his wife. "He certainly made dreadful films."

Bognor was being reflective. "I seem to spend a lot of

my life apprehending people who have done much-needed work," he said. "Getting rid of Silverburger was a service. He was a waste of space. And yet I am the instrument of a law that says that getting rid of him was wrong."

"*We* think he was a waste of space," said Monica, "but his mother must have loved him. And others. Not everyone thought of him as lowly as we do. Did. Besides killing people is wrong."

"I'm not so sure," said Bognor, recognizing that this was dangerous ground for an investigator. His role in life was defined and precise. The minute one started questioning it, one entered realms of philosophy and danger. His was not to reason why but simply to, well, get on with the job, and not ask too many questions. And he believed that what he was doing was right. He was the hammer of the righteous, the instrument of the law that ruled, and necessarily, the earth. Killing people was wrong. He knew and believed this as an article of absolute faith.

"Are you sure?" he asked, expecting an answer.

"What?" she said. "Sure about what? I don't deal in certainties. You know that. Or you jolly well ought to by now."

"Killing people," he said. "You said that killing people was wrong. Do you believe that?"

It was her turn to think for a while.

Eventually, she said quietly, "Like I said, I don't deal in certainties. But since you ask, most of the time, yes. And I think we have to live by that belief. But I'm not sure it's always right. Sorry...."

"Killing people is wrong," he said, "but sometimes killing people is better than not killing them. If people are a waste of space, we're better off without them."

"But"—she now seemed on surer ground—"that's not for us to decide, darling."

7

Eric Swanley's office was in London's Covent Garden. The garden itself was an unusual mixture of ancient and modern. Originally, it had been dedicated to vegetables, *Covent* being the old English for *convent* and the place being a sort of monks' garden for London during the reign of King John and for the following few hundred years. During Bognor's youth, it had been a glorified greengrocer, famous as much for its eccentric licensing laws as for its fruit and vegetables. Now it was a sort of theme park full of jugglers and cardsharps. The old buildings remained but had been transformed into trendy bars and cafés. Somehow, against most of the odds, it retained a bohemian, raffish atmosphere that Bognor liked.

Swanley's office was unreformed and gave the impression of having been well established when the first monkish gardeners originally arrived in the thirteenth century. There was no lift or elevator, and one ascended to the fifth floor by way of stone stairs. The walls were painted a pea green that Bognor associated with very old-fashioned public wards in run-down hospitals. Maybe urinals.

It was a suite of offices though that gave too extravagant and affluent an idea of them. Basically, there was an office in which Swanley worked and an outer area with a spinster of uncertain age hunched over a computer (one of the few concessions to modernity and an indicator that all was not entirely as it seemed). The chairs on which those waiting to be ushered into his presence were old-fashioned ladder-back dining room seats that gave the impression, like most of the fixtures and fittings, of having been there since the beginning.

Inside the main office, which Bognor was able to penetrate after an only marginal wait—just enough to convey business and importance but not enough to suggest indifference—the impression was one of paper. Paper was everywhere, mostly bundled and tied with ribbon, mostly pink. The paper, too, looked as if it came with the office as did Mr. Swanley himself.

"I've come about Mr. Silverburger," said Bognor.

"Of course. A tragic business. Alas, poor Irving." Swanley

rubbed his hands together, which produced a strange rasping noise, as if they were made from some kind of sandpaper. He offered Bognor a drink, suggesting a choice between tea and coffee, which his guest guessed was more apparent than real. Whatever he asked for would be warm, khaki-colored, and tasteless. He was surprised, therefore, when a serviceable large espresso arrived in a state-of-the-art Illy cup. That was, reflected Bognor, the new Covent Garden. He must remember that. All was not what it seemed. It never was, but looks, as so often, could be deceptive.

"He was a client of yours?"

"Indeed," said Swanley. "This is confidential, I take it."

Bognor agreed wondering as he did why Swanley was bothering to record it on a small, modern device. It probably did pictures as well. He was impressed.

Swanley wore an old-fashioned pinstriped suit. He looked and was behaving a little like the family undertaker. Only with twenty-first century trimmings like the recorder and the coffee. Bognor told himself to stay awake and not to think in terms of tape recorders and camp coffee.

"Had you known Mr. Silverburger long?" Bognor asked.

"Irving and I were like brothers," said Mr. Swanley, not answering the question nor appearing in the least German. *True Brit and smarmy with it*, thought Bognor.

"I'm delighted to hear it," he said, insincerely, "but how long had you been, er, brothers?"

"Irving started to spend more time in this country about a decade ago. I met him almost at once, and he became a client."

"And a brother?"

Swanley did not respond, and after a moment or so of stewing time, Bognor continued. "Do you mind telling me how you met?"

"Of course not," said Swanley. "We met through a mutual friend, an actress. Ingrid Vincent. She was in one of Irving's films."

"*The Coffee Grinders*," said Bognor.

"Yes," agreed the accountant looking ever so slightly surprised.

"Client?" asked Bognor.

"Yes."

"And sister?"

Mr. Swanley ignored this but said, "I tend to specialize in what people vulgarly call showbiz. I was with a bigger company—McPhersons. I seemed to look after their more creative clients. Then when we parted company, one or two came with me."

"I see," said Bognor. "When you say 'parted company,' what exactly does that mean?"

"Mutual consent," said Swanley, not looking guilty. "I know what you're implying but it was exactly as I describe. Entirely mutual. Our interests no longer coincided."

"I wouldn't dream of suggesting anything else," said Bognor, who was quite prepared to believe the worst, even if it was mutual. "But tell me about Ingrid Vincent."

"She's a client," he said. "A valued client. Came to me from McPhersons."

"But not particularly busy?" he asked. "Not apart from *The Coffee Grinders.*"

"I look after her finances, not her acting," the accountant said crisply. "I understand she's resting at the moment but, generally speaking, her income is healthy."

"Hmmm." Bognor frowned. He got the impression that Ingrid Vincent spent a lot of time "resting." She was a lady of leisure.

"Do you have many of your old clients from McPhersons days?"

"Not so many. To be absolutely honest, Irving kept me on my toes. Once I'd taken him on, it became difficult to do justice to anyone else. Even old friends from McPhersons days."

"Like Ingrid."

"If you insist. Like Ingrid."

Bognor decided on a change of tack.

"Venice mean anything to you?" he asked innocently.

"It was where Irving was murdered," said Swanley. "And oddly enough, it was the last place I saw him. He hosted a lunch at the new place on the other side of the canal. Near that hotel named after the architect. The Palladian. Lot of pillars. The wife and I had never been, and then suddenly these tickets came through the post. A cheapo airline but perfectly okay and a hotel room thrown in. All found. I didn't put two and two together until the lunch, and then I realized it must have been Irving. He was given to gestures like that. His idea of an office party. A sort of Christmas thrash except that it wasn't Christmas."

He smiled wanly, "Irving was a bit like that. Quixotic, you could say. That was what Ingrid said. She said not to ask questions."

The coffee was good. The proprietor, Mr. Illy, had been mayor of Trieste, which was, in a sense, next door to Venice, but a lot less glamorous and, to Bognor, almost preferable. Jan Morris had written about it affectionately, categorizing it as "nowhere" but approving it nonetheless. In fact, that was precisely why he liked it. No pressure. Nothing to see. Venice was almost too much.

"I'd been storing it up," said Mr. Swanley. "Top of my list. Not too far but full of all sorts of goodies. I mean I'd love to see the Grand Canyon and the Great Barrier Reef, but I just can't see the wife and me making that sort of journey. Not at our age. So Venice was, as I say, at the top of my list. In fact, I had it earmarked as a sort of retirement reward in a few years' time, but poor Irving beat us to it. I'm really sorry about what happened, but I'll always be grateful, too. And in a peculiar sort of way, there's no better place to go, wouldn't you agree? And I don't suppose he knew much about it. Here one moment, gone the next. And the last he will have seen was that wonderful place. I mean we all have to go sooner or later, and I'd rather it was in broad daylight in a boat in Venice than after hours in a National Health ward with tubes stuffed up every known aperture. Know what I mean?"

Bognor knew exactly what he meant, but that wasn't the point.

"So Irving paid for your tickets and your hotel?"

"I assume so," said Swanley. "Helen and I didn't . . . well, you know it wasn't like that. I assume he paid for the others at lunch. For Ingrid and for Trevor. Only he wasn't really Trevor, seeing as he was some sort of Balt. Came from Latvia. Somewhere outside Riga. I don't know what they're called there. Not Trevor anyway. We were all at the lunch. Us and the Eyeties."

"The Eyeties?"

"Irving's native friends. Benito, he was Italian, came across in a boat, I believe. And Sophia, only she was Russian. And the Pontis—Gina and Bernardo—and Father Carlo. I took a bit of a shine to Father Carlo. He was a Manchester City fan. Trautmann's old team. Know what I mean?"

Bognor knew what he meant. At least he thought he did. Any Mancunian worth his salt preferred the Sky Blues to the Red Devils, who were Manchester only in name, exercising a universal appeal whereas City, for all their foreign squillions—Thais, Svens, and now Saudis—were in some curious way, local. God knew why.

He was about to ask what they had eaten and drunk at Harry's Dolci but thought better of it. They would have drank some form of alcoholic peach juice since that was the Cipriani's stock in trade, and Silverburger and the restaurant would have ordered for them, which would have meant something safe but delicious, along the lines of a prosciutto or carpaccio panino and a *meringata* or chocolate torte. It would have been good but international. Nothing wrong with that but not the sort of food Brunetti would have had at Donna Leon's behest. Not Venetian but the sort of thing you could have got anywhere. At a price. That was Silverburger's style. Safe like McDonald's, only expensive. The best steak, the best *frites*, the best ketchup. Same everywhere he went: always the best table but always the same table.

"So it was friends of Irving Silverburger, old and new."

"You could say that," agreed Swanley. "Irving was like that. Always open to new experiences, new ideas, new people but amazingly loyal to those he trusted."

"Like you?"

"In a way like me, yes."

"But he paid."

Swanley went pink. "Yes," he said. "He paid and he paid well. But it wasn't like that. I would have gone to the wall for Irving. He knew that and I knew that. But it had nothing to do with money."

"Nevertheless," said Bognor, "he always paid his bills. And he was always on time. If he hadn't . . ."

"It didn't arise," said the accountant. "Like you say, Irving always settled immediately. On time. In full. No tick. It was part of what made him special."

Part of Bognor could not help wondering if it was the main thing that made the deceased special. But he didn't voice his suspicions.

"So Irving hosted lunch; and you think Irving paid for Trevor and Ingrid to come to Venice just as he paid for the two of you."

"That's a reasonable supposition," said Swanley. "But you

make it sound grubby, mercenary. It wasn't like that. We all liked Irving. Liked him a lot. And he liked us."

Bognor made a mental note not to be so cynical about everyone having a price, but these were mercenary times and he had lived through them. He would like to believe that those who lunched at Irving Silverburger's table in Venice liked him because of who he was and not because of what he gave them. All the same, he was suspicious. He believed that Silverburger's popularity was only paper thin and that the paper in this instance came in the form of bank notes. Or, because of where they were and who, the popularity was just so much pink plastic. He hoped he was wrong. In any case, he had to prove that the plastic was lethal and had a cutting edge. Also, that there were two sides to the card.

"Did you see Silverburger in Venice apart from the lunch at Harry's Dolci?"

"Absolutely not," said Swanley.

Did he say this a shade too quickly? Did he lack conviction? Bognor was not sure, but he felt uncomfortable.

"And Ingrid and Trevor? Did you know them? See them? Or the Italians?"

The accountant shook his head and looked as puzzled as Bognor was feeling. He seemed genuine enough, though and Bognor found himself feeling guilty for thinking otherwise. Swanley must have been good at his job, but had Bognor worked for Her Majesty's Revenue and Customs, he wouldn't have believed a word he said. Not a word.

"Thanks for the coffee and the chat," he said. "I'll see you at the funeral."

And he let himself out, shaking Mr. Swanley by the hand and inclining his head to the spinster crouched over the computer screen. She acknowledged him, just, with the slightest suspicion of a smile.

The funeral of Irving G. Silverburger was at the crematorium. It was raining. Actually, it was not rain in the acceptable tropical sense of a child's picture book with individual drops being thrown from an angry sky, but the thin apology that the English called, with a touch of xenophobia, Scotch mist. Bognor turned up the collar of his mackintosh and wondered why it always seemed to be foggy with damp whenever he came to the crem.

The coffin of Irving G. Silverburger was wheeled in professionally. The corpse of Irving G. Silverburger, which lay within, had been flown back from Italy and stayed in the fridgelike local morgue for some days waiting till today. After the usual more or less meaningless obsequies, the body would be burned and the alleged remains returned to the next of kin in a casket. They would then be taken home to the United States and disposed of. The dead man's only real memorial would probably be *The Coffee Grinders*, which didn't count for much. It would probably turn up as a tricky University Challenge question in a few years' time. A latter day quizmaster with a piercing stare and a strangulated voice would ask a pimply youth who had produced *The Coffee Grinders*, and he would answer, "Irving G. Silverburger." There would be wild applause, and the trophy would duly make its way to some dim college in a new university of which few people knew as much as they did even about the works of the late and unlamented Silverburger.

Bognor sat at the back. This was his preferred position on occasions such as this. It had the combined benefit of rendering him less noticeable if not actually invisible and enabling him to watch. He was not a participant. He seldom was. His role in life was, he thought, essential, but also peripheral. It always had been and though this had worried him and more obviously Monica in earlier years he had become used to it, as had his wife, though less obviously so.

This time, he was with Contractor. Apart from them, the congregation, which was thin, consisted almost entirely of the usual suspects.

He recognized Swanley, aka Braun, who was accompanied by a sniveling woman, presumably his wife, and wore the same suit but a different tie. At least, thought Bognor, it looked like the same suit but Swanley was the sort of man who would have a number of identical-looking suits not wishing to seem different for fear of frightening the horses. It was almost as important for Swanley to be unobtrusive and unthreatening as it was for Bognor. Bognor recognized this but also sensed that it suited Swanley's temperament. Swanley was the sort of man who did not like to be the center of attention.

There was no escaping it this time for he gave one of the two addresses. One was from a cousin who had come from the American Midwest and was anonymous in a wholesome way, but the other was Swanley.

"I never knew the *G* stood for Giovanni," Bognor whispered to Contractor. "Italian blood would explain a lot. If Silverburger was Italian . . . the Tuscan Silverburgers . . . the Calabrian Silverburgers . . . Silverburgani."

"His parents probably just dug opera," Contractor said prosaically. "Nothing in Idaho except potatoes and seventy-eights."

"Who said his people came from Idaho?" asked Bognor. "I thought it was Iowa. Or somewhere else."

"Somewhere between the Eastern seaboard and California. It's all much of a muchness. I think a family love of opera is more likely than Italian blood. Sorry."

They sang "Cwm Rhondda." At least the organist played "Cwm Rhondda," and the choir on the DVD accompanied her. The congregation shuffled from foot to foot, looked embarrassed and in a very few cases hummed. It would be pushing the envelope to claim that anybody actually sang.

After "Cwm Rhondda," there was a reading from the Old Testament by someone Bognor guessed was the factotum from Riga who styled himself Trevor. He read satisfactorily enough, in the manner of one who had studied English as a foreign language under the tuition of similarly taught foreigners at a language school in a seedy resort on the impoverished East Coast. His mastery of English was greater than that of many natives, but it was obviously not his own mother tongue, something he had picked up along the way and that he made use of because it suited him.

The clergyman had obviously not known the deceased and didn't care. He was the ecclesiastical equivalent of a lawyer provided by Legal Aid. He would draw the miserable minimum and go through the miserable minimum motions. He stumbled over Silverburger's name and rattled through the formulaic prayers with all the passion of a peanut. Bognor should have felt sorry for the man, but felt only contempt. He wasn't even doing his job.

To say that Swanley lifted proceedings would have been overstating the case, but he did at least give the impression that he knew who the dead man was and that if not exactly sorry that he had died would at least have preferred him to have been alive. Perhaps that was no more than professional self-interest, but Bognor felt it was slightly more, and he was moved by the man's evident sorrow.

"There's no point in pretending," he began, and looked around the bleak little room, his gaze lingering for a moment on the box in which the remains of Irving G. Silverburger lay ready to enter the flames of the industrial furnace fueled at council expense, consuming all manner of folk. "No point in pretending anything very much, least of all that our friend, Irving, was the most popular of men. Had he been widely loved and appreciated, had he been the life and soul of the party, had he been generous and selfless then, perhaps, there would have been more of us present to mark his passing. And yet there is something to be said for the paucity of numbers. We who mourn Irving are an exclusive band. There are not many of us."

This was obviously true. There were the paid, namely the vicar and undertakers' people; the family, a handful of embarrassed folks from the American Midwest who were there out of a sense of duty and obligation but had no feelings of real loss or sorrow; and the friends. Heaven alone knows what the friends were feeling and it would have been odd if they felt anything approaching the same. Each one had his own memories. Some might have been genuinely fond of Irving, though Bognor found this hard, on what little evidence he possessed, to believe.

Swanley was still speaking. "Many of us," he said, "were present at that last lunch. We did not realize at the time that it was to be a last lunch any more than the disciples realized that the meal with Our Lord was to be the Last Supper."

Bognor, who had been brought up in a correct, if unbelieving, Church of England fashion, felt a tremor of embarrassment. It was the height of bad taste to mention Jesus Christ and Irving Silverburger in the same paragraph. Not accurate, either. Or called for.

Some members of the congregations of his youth would have walked out.

"I don't think Irving thought it was a last lunch. Instead, he wanted to celebrate friendship. No more and no less. That is what he would wish us to do today. For as the writer said, 'He is not dead but just gone into the next room.' It's the same with Irving. He is with us and we are with him. He is not dead but sleepeth. We hear his laugh; we feel his hand-shake; we sense his love."

And that was it.

"Bad theology," said Bognor. "Death means what it says. Everyone agrees about that—the pope, Richard Dawkins. It's not an issue to serious theologians."

"Dawkins isn't a theologian," Contractor hissed in protest.

"Oh yes, he is," said Bognor. "He's just an atheist theologian."

They sang "The Day Thou Gavest," which they would have made sound more dirgelike than usual if humming could be thought funereal; then a weedy cousin, jet-lagged, overawed, mouthed banalities and said the family would be happy to see friends for a drink and a sandwich at a pub on the riverside at Richmond-on-Thames five minutes' drive away and then the on-duty priest rattled through a few banalities before Silverburger's box went trundling through the curtains into the all-consuming flames.

Production line, thought Bognor in a thought he did not share even with his subordinate. He had no idea how he wished to be disposed of though, as he wouldn't be alive to take part, he didn't feel he was entitled to particular views on the subject. But he did not wish to go like this: burial at sea, scattered from a balloon—anything but a ritual burning with a rent-a-priest and a bored congregation present out of a misplaced sense of duty and the hope of a free drink and a tired sandwich.

No, he thought, *that was unfair.* There was, surprisingly, a decent amount of genuine grief. There were people here who were sorry to see the last of Irving Giovanni Silverburger. One of them had probably, possibly, killed him, and he or she was also doing a passable imitation of sorrow. But then one did. They could be crocodile tears, but Bognor's experience was that not only did killers cry, they wept tears of genuine regret. The murder hurt them more than it hurt the victim.

They hummed "Thine Be the Glory," and the organist played some sort of all-purpose theme on a tune by Bach. Well, it *was* a rent-a-fugue. Outside, it was still raining or still wet. The damp enveloped the crematorium and the surrounding cemetery in a thin pall of dank mist, lowering spirits that were already ankle-low. Bognor and Contractor walked slowly to the waiting Rover, one of the last made in Britain, a sort of misplaced flamboyance, which sent out all sorts of wrong message. Comfortable though. Bognor told the driver to drop them at the riverside, have something for his own lunch and pick them up after an hour. Contractor said nothing, just did as he was told. This was not a time for dissent or even discussion.

It was still misty by the Thames, but the rain had stopped, and a pale sun was even trying forlornly to penetrate the gloom. Ducks and swans fought in a desultory way over crusts and the ends of sandwiches thrown into the river by mainly foreign lunchers.

Contractor bought a couple of pints of Courage Directors Bitter, paid for them himself, promised to claim them back on his expenses and joined the boss on the wide towpath. There seemed nothing to say and they both said it; staring morosely over the froth at the top of their drinks toward Twickenham on the opposite bank. Bognor guessed it would be sunnier in Venice. It nearly always was. At least in his mind's eye.

"I think we should have a word with Trevor the Balt," said Bognor, nodding in the direction of the thin chauffeur's suit sipping a Virgin or maybe Bloody Mary on his own. "He looks as if he could use company."

Contractor grinned, and the two men walked over to Trevor where they introduced themselves. Trevor's response was noncommittal. He wasn't cold, let alone frosty, but he wasn't warm, let alone welcoming. Neutral.

"It's a free country," he said when Bognor asked if he would mind dreadfully if he and his colleague were to ask one or two questions.

"Meaning Latvia wasn't?" Contractor said sharply.

"I didn't say that," Trevor said equally sharply. "But since you ask, no. Not when I left. Far from it. And I will always be grateful to Irving for his help. If it hadn't been for him, I'd never have made it. Or I'd be living rough in Wisbech, picking tulips for a subsistence wage. Or cockling near Morecambe Bay."

"Silverburger helped with your visa?" asked Bognor.

"It's all past history now. And the situation's changed. Latvia's not the same. None of those places are. Stag parties. I've been back. Not a problem. When I first came, there was no going back."

He took a sip of his tomato and repeated, "No going back."

"So you were old friends?" This from Contractor.

"Not at all," said Trevor. "Didn't know him from a bar of soap. Noticed his name in a fleapit in downtown Riga. He rolled around on the credits, and I'd liked the movie. Sort of. So I wrote to him, and to my amazement he wrote back." Trevor smiled. "So I'll always be grateful despite, well, despite . . ."

"The film," said Contractor. "Which one was it?"

"There only ever was one really," said Trevor. He looked wistful. "*The Coffee Grinders*," he said.

"So," said Bognor, "I'm going to have to watch that ghastly film?"

Contractor smiled. "I'm afraid so, Boss. We can book a viewing theater if it would make it any easier. Or just get a DVD."

"Book a theater." He didn't often go for the extravagance to which his job and title entitled him. Indeed, he belonged, if not to the hair-shirt style of boss at least to the bicycling variety. Had he been a king, he would have traveled at the back of the bus and been roundly vilified by those who believed that monarchy was largely to do with pomp and circumstance. Basically, Bognor was neither into pomp nor circumstance. Faced, however, with the purgatory of having to watch a movie, which he dimly remembered having to sit through on a previous occasion, he felt he was entitled.

The encounter with Trevor had yielded nothing beyond formalities. Indeed, Bognor could scarcely say that the funeral generally had thrown up anything new in terms of evidence unless one counted the realization that, to a very select few, Silverburger was not such a bad egg after all. Indeed, there were those, mostly in the crem that morning, who thought Silverburger was rather a good egg. Or at least they knew which side their toast was buttered.

Had it not been for Irving G., Trevor would still be in Latvia or under a hedge in Wisbech. Instead of this, he was buttling in Belgravia, lapped in luxury with nothing much to do except serve the man who had released him from a life as a Soviet serf.

In his Latvian life, he had been Artis Dombrovskis. There were lots of sibilances in Latvian life, mostly at the end of people's names, first and second. A Latvian Fred or Bert would have been Freds or Berts. Dombrovkis was the name of the prime minister, but Artis, aka Trevor, was no relation. He should have been Trevors and he should have been subjected to more rigorous questioning. Some other time perhaps.

Meanwhile he *had* been to Venice; he *had* been staying at the Danieli, albeit in a broom cupboard while his employer had a suite. And while he *had* done some servanting, he had been on a longish leash. Much of the time, he had behaved like any other tourist from a Baltic state: badly and independently.

That was the extent of Trevor's revealing admission. He had been in Venice at Silverburger's expense and in a sense at his beck and call. He, therefore, had the opportunity. He had not been in the same water taxi and was not on the same flight, which in the case of Silverburger was a scheduled British Airways flight for which he had a first-class ticket. He was a frequent flier with BA.

"I suppose," said Bognor, "there *was* a motive."

"Sorry, Boss," said Contractor. "You're suggesting our man was killed for no particular reason."

"Well," said Bognor, "kicks, if you call that a reason."

"You mean someone went and killed him because they liked killing people."

"Happens," said Bognor. "Happens all the time as a matter of fact. Doesn't get reported for two good reasons. One is that it would alarm people. The second is that such a vague motive makes it very difficult to solve."

"Motiveless murder?" Contractor mused. "Seems a bit of a waste when there were so many good reasons for wanting Silverburger dead. Random killing accounts for the good, not the evil. Really unpleasant people such as Silverburger don't happen to get done in. They're murdered on purpose."

"I wouldn't be so sure," said Bognor. "Why shouldn't some fruitcake with a crossbow just wander out one day with murder on his mind and find that our friend presented the ideal target? I feel like that sometimes."

Contractor looked at his boss with a new and different eye. He had not previously thought that he could be working for a killer.

"Let's face it," Bognor warmed to his theme, "if we thought we could get away with it, many more of us would be murderers. That's why I'm glad there are sanctions. Otherwise, I might have murdered Monica. Several times. And vice versa. And in the fullness of time, I'd have regretted it. So, I think would she. Ditto Parkinson, my boss in former times. I daresay you could have cheerfully killed me from time to time. I could certainly have killed you on numerous occasions. But, on balance and up to a point, one would have regretted it in the morning."

"Yes." It was Contractor's turn to be fazed. He had heard of Parkinson. Frequently. He sounded like a dry, old stick and very much of his time. Maybe another law of life was that one grew into one's boss. He shuddered and hoped not.

"What has emerged from our end," he said, "is that Silverburger was not as nasty as he appeared. Or rather that he had people who appeared to be quite fond of him. Not many but genuinely fond. We have a short list of such people and we now know that Trevor and the Swanleys were in the Venice area at the time of Silverburger's death. On the other hand, there seems to be less and less reason for the Swanleys or Trevor the Balt to have killed him. Not only did they like him but he was a goose laying golden eggs all the time. Why would they want to kill him? He was their emotional friend and their financial benefactor. Two good reasons for wanting him alive. Dead and the first vanishes and the second does so effectively as well. Whatever money there may have been goes back to the American Midwest, never to be seen again. So Trevor and Swanley are up a gum tree in every conceivable sense."

"Which leaves La Vincent."

"Which leaves La Vincent," agreed Bognor.

"She was at the funeral."

Bognor recalled an anonymous figure in a black coat, some sort of animal around her throat, and a theatrical veil attached to a black hat with a big brim. There was a lot of sniffing of a theatrical nature, which seemed to say, "Look at me, I'm suffering," and he hadn't see her by the Thames at the wake. No car. She had probably used public transport. He knew nothing about her apart from what he was about to discover from his viewing of *The Coffee Grinders*.

"Yes," he said.

"The Pontis sort of come within our remit," said Contractor, "in their Northamptonshire incarnation."

"I'll talk to Michael about them," he said, and asked Contractor when he could arrange a viewing of Silverburger's film. Silly question. The answer was the day before yesterday. Contractor knew people. He could fix a little place in Wardour Street; no problem getting a print; was Sir Simon doing anything this evening? Perhaps Lady Bognor would like to come. He would see if Sam was up for it. They could have a meal afterward. Could be quite fun. They should make something out of it. The movie couldn't be *that* bad.

"Yes, it could," said Bognor. He had seen a fair number of spaghetti-nothings. He knew how bad they could be and he feared the worst.

8

The surroundings could be compensation, though, and the Global Moviedrome in Wardour Square was a case in point. The tiny theater was not a lot bigger than Bognor's office at SIDBOT, but it contained a dozen or so armchairs and armrests with room for food and drink. There was a pretty blonde at the front of house to take their coats and dish out big gin-and-tonics with loads of ice clanking against the sides of crystal. The chips were handcrafted from root vegetables other than potatoes. If one had to watch films such as *The Coffee Grinders*, then this was the place to do so. Perhaps, he thought, that was why so much execrable celluloid was unleashed. Critical faculties were suspended. Distribution was about the size of one's gin and the depth of the armchair. Nothing to do with the film.

Monica was present; equine, adorable, love of his life, tiresome, difficult, argumentative, but his wife. Sam was also there. She fulfilled much the same role for Contractor and the two women shared a disdainful, eye-rolling love of their men, which meant that they gravitated to each other and were the bane of everybody's lives (not least of their husbands', both of whom adored them to bits but were damned if they would acknowledge this, particularly in public). Sam was socially grander than Contractor, just as Monica was out of a higher drawer than Bognor. Sam was also white, unlike her husband. This sometimes caused problems but less and less so. In some quarters, it was thought positively chic, whereas the monochrome Bognor union was regarded as sadly old-fashioned.

The four of them were the only audience.

Bognor supposed he had seen the film before. It was bad in every possible respect from the tin-eared script to the myopic camerawork, the plywood and balsa-wood acting and the resolutely mundane special effects. There was nothing special about these and nothing out of the ordinary about the movie as a whole. It didn't even have the guts to be truly ghastly but came in at a bad beta in every respect.

Bognor wondered if he could sleep through the thing but was afraid he might snore. It was bad enough not to be alert throughout the performance but beyond redemption to prevent the others from nodding off. The distaff side, for instance, had no professional reason for being present. They were only there to support their husbands.

It was a bad print, flickering and speckled with orange spots. The credits said "Introducing Ingrid Vincent," which was a bit of a laugh as she had never needed an introduction in real life and had not, as far as he was aware, followed up the introduction with any further forays in her professional life. Once introduced, she had apparently languished like a thespian wallflower. He supposed she could have had vampish parts in elderly drawing room comedies in seedy rep companies, but he suspected she would have drawn the line at such stuff of the theatrical art. She was not a trouper, just a tart.

He was thinking along these lines when she was "introduced" for the first time, wearing an absurdly tight roll-necked sweater that showed off her ample breasts. He wondered idly if they were artificially enhanced or if they grew big naturally in Cluj-Napoca, where she came from, according to her file, which was thin and which he had read several times from cover to cover. She was working a huge, hissy Gaggia machine in an old-fashioned coffee bar, somewhere ill defined but probably British.

She did not have many words, which was just as well as she was not easy to understand. However, she was not there to speak but to flutter her Barbara Cartland–style eyelashes, pout prettily, and bare her ample bosom. Actually, she wouldn't bare her bosom because had she done so the movie would have been denied a certificate. Also she would have prostituted what she liked to call her "art." She was not going to do either but simply fluttered, pouted, and said as little as possible while silhouetted provocatively behind the suggestively steamy coffee machine.

The film had a plot of sorts. It involved a murder, maybe more than one. There were cops, good guys, and bad guys. The bad guys were very bad and very visual about it, wearing black and affecting thin false mustaches and mock Italian accents. The good guys had lantern jaws and piercing blue contact lenses of a kind nobody wore in real life. Nobody could act, which was just as well as it was not required and would have been noticed and thought poncy and pretentious. Nobody could speak properly, which was just as well as the only lines were clichés.

Ingrid was a moll, but no one, including Ingrid, seemed entirely sure whose moll she was. She was either a good guy's girl or a bad guy's Sheila; either had a heart of gold or of stone. But nobody seemed to know. This was acceptable, but no one cared, which was worse. And it didn't seem to matter, which was inexcusable.

From time to time, however, when words failed her, which was often, she kissed whatever male was in the vicinity. She was good at this and had obviously had practice.

During one particularly steamy embrace behind the Gaggia, Bognor let out a sudden squeal of recognition.

"Freeze," he said. "Stop the film. I know that person. He's not supposed to be here. Not yet. But I know him."

It was Trevor. Trevors. Or Altis Dombrovskis. The Balt

butler. The manservant from Latvia. He was younger than this morning, and he was wearing winklepickers and tight trousers. Like Ingrid, he was a mean kisser. They were in a clinch that looked as if they meant it. In fact, it was the only meaningful part of the film

"Who is he?" Monica whispered loudly, and said nothing when he explained, simply ate another peanut and looked at her husband wistfully. Bognor told the projectionist to unfreeze the frame and go back to forward. Trevor duly vanished never to be seen again, killed offscreen by one of the bad guys who was eventually apprehended and duly swung, the film being set in a country where they still had capital punishment. Still, the man in the clinch was Trevor. Of that much, Bognor was certain.

So Trevor from Riga was in the United Kingdom when he shouldn't have been, when he said he wasn't, and long before he admitted to having met Silverburger. And he was a good kisser. On-screen and when the object of his *tendresse* was an older woman. None of this made him a murderer. It made him a liar for reasons as yet unknown. It made him a decent kisser who presumably knew Ingrid Vincent. Not that the knowledge may have been more than skin-deep as it were. La Vincent, after all, was an introducee, which was the next best thing to a star, whereas Trevor was little more than an extra, a walk-on kisser. The characters they portrayed may have known each other intimately, but the actor and actress may not have known each other at all. They were simply creatures that kissed on screen.

The rest of the film told Bognor nothing new about Trevor, aka Artis, for the good reason that his appearance was fleeting, if sensuous. It should have told Bognor a lot about the pulchritudinous Pupescu, but although he managed to stay awake throughout the movie, he didn't learn a great deal about Ingrid except that she looked good and reacted enthusiastically to the attentions of males. She was, in an old-fashioned phrase, "a sex kitten." She resembled former film stars such as Anita Ekberg and Zsa Zsa Gabor. She was well endowed, keen on sexual contact, had a sultry foreign accent, which contributed to her mystery and allure, and she couldn't act.

"Is that Ingrid's own voice?" he asked innocently.

There was a chorus of incredulous disbelief in which the implied subtext was that he was someone who didn't understand film and was out of touch.

"Natalie Wood's singing voice was dubbed in *West Side Story* and Audrey Hepburn's in *My Fair Lady*," said Bognor. "They looked good, but they couldn't sing. So they used their voice coach. She looked like the back of a bus, but she sang like a lark."

"Ingrid doesn't sing," said his wife.

"But she talks," said Bognor, "and she can't. If you see what I mean."

"Oh, Simon," she said. "Honestly!"

Bognor still thought his question was valid, but the others were so derisory that he shut up. They all obviously knew much more about film and its conventions than he did. He was not, he was the first to concede, a cinematic animal. He understood books, the theater, and old-fashioned stories in a general, traditional sort of a way. He liked beginnings and middles and ends, plausible characters and recognizable plots. Being entertained and kept on his toes was part of the game and he liked to be stretched even if the stretching was comfortable in the style of a *Times* crossword rather than the rack. He was not there to be improved but he was not interested in escapism, either.

Film performed this function though not, on the whole, modern film. He enjoyed John Wayne and Gary Cooper, and if asked to name his favorite movies of all time, would probably have settled for *Casablanca*, *High Noon*, or most of the films from the Ealing Comedies series. His tastes were therefore conservative but not stupid. *The Coffee Grinders* was modern and mindless and therefore he hated it.

On the other hand, he recognized that watching it was part of his job and not simply a pleasure. The unexpected appearance of Trevor the Balt was a bonus and otherwise he was supposed to study Ingrid Vincent. This he did, finding it no hardship at all, undemanding but ultimately unsatisfying. There was something about her that was not quite right: an artificial quality that should have been at home on film but left one feeling cheated. She was like a bad Indian meal.

"What did you think?" Bognor asked in a general way, not expecting any very coherent answer.

Contractor said something unintelligible about cinematography, auteurs, and camera angles. Sam went pink and seemed to agree. Monica said, "Just what you'd expect. Not even bad enough to be rubbish."

These were Bognor's own thoughts.

"And yet he was always described as 'film producer' as if he was good at it," said Bognor. "I don't understand."

"If you repeat something often enough and loudly enough, people will begin to believe you. Silverburger told everyone he was a film producer, and after a while they started to believe him. Same with Ingrid. She told everyone she was a film star, and after a while, that's how she was described and how she was known. I think she began to believe it herself. And in a macabre way, she was right. She may not actually have been a film star, but she should have been and this was recognized, so she became one. It's commonplace. If you believe something enough, it will come true, particularly if you say it very slowly and very loudly."

That was it really. The film was ordinary; La Vincent likewise. Both had large sums of money expended on them; both were told they were not second-rate despite overwhelming evidence to the contrary; and both vanished virtually without trace after their brief moment in the twilight.

"Has she ever worked again?" Bognor wanted to know, and the consensus was that she had made one or two advertisements, including an almost famous one on behalf of the English asparagus growers from the Vale of Evesham. Mostly, however, she had been reduced to opening supermarkets and appearing in celebrity game shows, which had their origin in Japan and featured people such as herself who were not particularly celebrated for being not particularly celebrated. She was often mentioned in gossip columns, usually when there was no one else to write about and a journalist or two were feeling particularly jaded. Ingrid Vincent was a victim of celebrity culture, being neither celebrated nor cultured but having to make do in an ersatz world where nobody would have recognized the real McCoy anyway and where, ultimately, no one much cared.

Bognor had a sudden craving for a hamburger with American mustard and a number of highly colored relishes together with some German-based beer from Milwaukee. This was available in Soho like most foreign dishes, and the other three joined him, Contractor observing that since they had spent a couple of hours being bored rigid by foreign dishes he saw no reason to be otherwise for the rest of the evening. If he was going to be gastronomically threatened, he would like to see the threat carried out.

"I suppose I should talk to her," he said wearily, chin streaked with loud color.

"Of course," agreed the others, not really seeing the point but conforming to the rules of the game. Even if one ignored them in the end, it was important to be seen to be observing them most of the time. Enemies noticed such things and would be quick to take advantage of errors or omissions. And Bognor and SIDBOT had plenty of enemies.

He and Monica walked home, which was possible, saved money, and promoted the illusion of well-being, compensating for the gin and the burger. They liked the city after hours. Even the rattle and clunk of garbage trucks doing whatever they did to empty bottles had a louche, extramural sound and smell. Waste, dirt, stubbly men with large dogs laid out in doorways surrounded by rags and a cardboard box had an appeal. The place stank of people living close to one another, exchanging unmentionable fluids and odors. Anonymity and loneliness stalked the streets and lurked on corners; everyone was foreign and came from some-where else; this was urban living, and it was what Simon and Monica had opted for many years ago. They relished the edge, the menace, the danger, and took pleasure in the lack of security and the imminence of sudden death. Urban crime was more thoughtless and less premeditated than its country cousin, and they were used to its changes of pace, its lack of rhythm, its sudden shifts. They were town mice; rats, at home with gutters and dirt.

"Couldn't live anywhere but London," said Monica, gaz-ing at the all-enveloping squalor and inhaling the stench of the stale, the discarded, and the unwanted. "Imagine being clean."

"Singapore," said Bognor. "Like school. Penalties for lit-tering. Big Brother and Sister always watching and listening and telling you what to do. Everyone knowing each other's business and minding it."

Monica neatly sidestepped a fallen drunk lying across her path.

"That was a fantastically forgettable film," she said. "Must have cost a fortune. And that nubile tartlet, the Transylvanian totty . . . rumpy-dumpy from Romania. I suppose your friend Mr. Silverburger had his wicked way with her."

"I suppose so," said Bognor, who hadn't really given the matter a lot of thought but supposed so now that Monica had mentioned it.

"Do you think that's enough to constitute a murder motive?"

"Going to bed with the producer/director?"

"And then being rejected."

"Rejected? Who said she was rejected?"

"She hadn't acted in a film since *The Coffee Grinders.*"

"But Irving hadn't made a movie since *The Coffee Grinders.*"

"No."

They walked across Wigmore Street in silence.

"Do you imagine it had anything to do with cause and effect?" mused Bognor. "I mean do you imagine that Silverburger didn't make any more movies because of Ingrid?"

"Because he insisted on having her in any sequel? Or because he ditched her?"

"Either," said Bognor, "or both. We'll never know if he slept with her. If he threw her out. Was still with her. Wanted to hire her for a new movie. Had got rid of her. The secret died with him. We'll never know."

"You could ask her," said Monica. They were passing an old Greek restaurant where they did a mean moussaka, dispensed pepper from gunmetal grinders, and served a house retsina that stripped linings and even a banker's assets at a hundred paces. Or something like that. Why was commercial *taramasalata* so vividly pink? Bognor wished he knew the answer. Why did everybody seem to think you had to be so heavy-handed with the cochineal when the real article was so visually lackluster?

"Do you really think she's two-a-penny?" he asked. "That there are hundreds just like her? East European tartlets on the make. Sleeping their way to what they hope will be the top because it's all they have."

"All they think they have," said Monica. "Doesn't make any odds. If you have the misfortune to be a female from the old Communist empire, you're only good for sex. You're there to be trafficked. Doesn't matter if you're Einstein, the male only wants what's between your legs."

Bognor was shocked.

"Don't," he said. "It's not nice. Nor true."

"It may not be nice, but it's certainly true. Even in the so-called civilized West, we have glass ceilings everywhere. Little ladies have their place, which is in bed, rocking the cradle, or maybe at the sink or stove. Certainly, not in an advantageous position at the boardroom table."

"And Ingrid wasn't Einstein?"

He felt Monica shrug. "Maybe, maybe not. Couldn't act for toffee."

"So was she a killer?"

"That's for you to find out," she said. "You'll have to ask her. You never know. She might tell you."

They had arrived at their front door. Between the Indian newsagent and the dry cleaners.

Bognor got out his key and unlocked the door.

"I'll have to do the interview. Can't say I'm looking forward to it."

"Liar," said Monica, kissing him as they entered the elevator. It had been there for a long time. Its doors creaked and it rattled. One day, it might kill someone, but so far it never had. One day, though. Perhaps it would plunge to the basement with a passenger inside.

He kissed her back, and they went rattling upward, happy after their own fashion.

9

Ingrid Vincent, née Pupescu, lived in a mansion block over-looking the Thames at Kingston. It was close to the for-mer film studios at Teddington, latterly the production HQ for Thames TV and a place to which the actress felt she belonged though she never quite did. It dropped nicely into her conversation, though.

Nobody knew for certain quite how old Ingrid was. Like a Pakistani cricketer, she arrived in Britain with no verifiable birth certificate and she was almost certainly older than she made out. At the time, it didn't matter, and she got away with it. Everyone knew that she was mutton dressed as lamb, but she was a passable sheep and, hey, who cared?

She appeared in *The Coffee Grinders,* which may have been ghastly but was more than most of her competitors managed, and for a while, she was seen on the right arms and at the right parties. When she said that she was an actress, nobody gainsayed her. Maybe they believed her; maybe they couldn't be bothered; maybe they were frightened by her often-criminal squires. But at any event, she became a popular girl about town with fashionably lax morals and prominent breasts, which she was not afraid to flaunt.

Latterly, however, she had faded. *Faded blonde* were the words commonly used, and the cloche fitted like the proverbial glove. At dueling space, she still looked good, for she had kept her figure and her bone structure was a guarantee of approving verdicts on the height of cheekbones, the gamineness of expression and the general pertness, which belied the years at a distance. Closer, you caught the lines and wrinkles around the neck and wrists. These were the unmistakable signs of advancing years and gave the lie to the extravagant makeup and the pert expression. It was unfair, meant different things to different sexes and rendered Ingrid increasingly ridiculous. She was not growing old gracefully. She refused to concede that she was growing old at all, and *graceful* was not in her vocabulary.

Most of this Bognor guessed, if he did not already know it. Much of it was in his briefing document; the rest was in his brain masquerading as prejudice. Nevertheless, he had to see for himself and measure the reality against what he thought, what he felt, and what he had read. Thus the tube to Wimbledon and a bus to Kingston, a brisk walk, and a ring on the doorbell. He had rung ahead so that she was prepared, but why not? Neither had anything to hide, and the dawn raid by the security police kicking in the front door and taking the inhabitant away without anyone having the first idea what was going on had died, surely, with the Ceauşescus.

She had a miniature poodle. It was old and smelly, and she called it Charley's Aunt, and carried it under her arm when she opened her door. She smelled of cheap scent and alcohol; the dog of urine.

"Sir Simon," she said, "please come in. Don't mind Charley's Aunt."

Charley's Aunt snuffled and snarled. Bognor put out a hand, but this seemed to agitate the dog and increased the decibel rating. He withdrew and smiled instead.

The flat was sad in an indefinable way, made the more so by the occupier's indefatigable chirpiness; an optimism that Bognor felt was false and could easily be defeated. It was old-fashioned with chintz and prints, and it smelled of the smells he had caught when she opened the door but also, just, of mothballs and cooking. Or was that simply his imagination? Nice view and a tiny balcony. Too cold to sit out, though.

She offered him a gin, which she had obviously been at already, lit a cigarette, sat down on the sofa, crossed her legs, adjusted her pantyhose, and smiled a tight little smile, which almost broke his heart though not for reasons she intended.

"So what can I do for you? I presume it's about Irving."

There was a picture of the dead man on a table in a silver frame, signed and smiling. He looked smarmy, which was usual, but she seemed neither to notice nor mind.

"Were you in Venice the other day?" he asked, not seeing any need to avoid the point and wanting to get everything over with as soon as possible. He wanted to leave.

"Yes," she said. She evidently saw no need to avoid the point either, but she wanted him to stay. She welcomed the distraction. Hers had become a boring and disappointing life. "Irving must have paid for my ticket and the hotel, but nothing was said. He wasn't like that."

Her English, thought Bognor, had improved since *The Coffee Grinders*. It was still heavily accented but syntactically much better.

"Where did you stay? How did you fly?"

"I went by easyJet," she said. "But it is a short flight, and the plane goes to the main airport, so there was no problem. Marco Polo. It is named after a famous Italian explorer. The hotel was small but clean, central. I forget the name, but I can find it if you wish. The Pensione something. It was okay. And we had one lunch together. Irving and all his friends. On the other side of the canal. Nice. Very expensive. Very stylish. Very Irving." She smiled. Wistfully. An aging spinster on the outside with a little girl inside trying still to get out. Bognor thought smugly that it was different for men, different perhaps for a different sort of woman. Monica, for instance. Perhaps it was necessary to be alone to seem like this: so vulnerable. He wondered if there had originally been a relationship between her and Silverburger and whether and on what terms the relationship had persisted.

"Good lunch?"

She smiled.

"Very good lunch. I would say not especially Italian, but Irving was a citizen of the world not of a particular place, so he ate the world's food and he expected his guests to do the same."

It was on the tip of his tongue to say that you could learn a lot from gastronomy and that perhaps Napoleon had a point when he maintained that an army marched on its stomach. But then maybe Napoleon was talking figuratively and, in any case, he wasn't really French, and Corsican food and civilization was its own thing and not the same as on the mainland. But Bognor remembered where he was and what he was supposed to be doing, so he smiled and nodded and asked if she could remember what she had had.

"A cocktail," she said, "wine, prosciutto, pasta, some sort of pudding, grappa. Good. Good company. Irving's friends. There was hope in the air. The sight of a new movie. With Irving, there was always the hope of a new movie, but this time it was real."

"*The Lemon Peelers?*"

She inclined her head. "That was what he called the idea. It was to be a sequel to *The Coffee Grinders.*"

"And you were going to have a starring role again?"

"Yes," she said. Her glass was empty, and she refilled it

from a Gordon's bottle. It was cloudy with Schweppes Bitter Lemon, but there was not much of it, whereas there was a lot of Gordon's. Bognor noticed but made no comment.

"What about Gina Ponti?"

"What about Gina Ponti?"

It was the same question, but Ingrid gave it novelty value by emphasizing the *about*. This had the effect of making it a different sentence.

"My understanding was that Bernardo Ponti was going to finance the project on condition that Gina had a big part."

This may have been his understanding, but it had not hitherto been voiced even by Dibdini, who nevertheless thought it as well. Bernardo had access to funds, and Gina harbored thespian ambitions. It didn't require much ingenuity to put two and two together and come up with this theory.

"Gina has no experience. She cannot act. *Pouf!*"

The dog had made an excruciating smell and now whimpered. Bognor and her mistress pretended not to notice.

"But Bernardo had money . . ." said Bognor.

"So Bernardo had money," she said. "So what if Bernardo had money? What difference does that make?"

"A lot of difference I'm afraid," said Bognor. "There is a saying in England that 'money makes the world go round' and it is, alas, surprisingly true. A movie costs a great deal of money to make. A great deal. And Irving Silverburger did not have money of his own. He needed to do what is called 'raise capital' to make a movie such as *The Lemon Peelers* become possible. And maybe Gina Ponti was the price for Bernardo making his money available."

At first, Ingrid said nothing but stubbed out a cigarette angrily, causing the dog to whimper again.

"You have other sayings," she then said. "You have 'there is more to life than money.'"

"We have many sayings involving money," said Bognor, trying to be gentle. "There is another that says that 'every man has his price.' Perhaps Gina was the price that Mr. Silverburger was going to have to pay."

"Not possible," she said.

"But you must understand if the price Irving Silverburger had to pay was Gina, then that gives you a very good motive for killing him."

"But why should I kill him?" she asked. "He was my friend. I had good reason for killing that talentless bitch Gina and maybe her husband as well, but I had no reason whatever for killing Irving. No Irving, no movie. No movie, no future. His death killed hope."

This was not only almost poetic; it was probably true. Silverburger was probably her only prospective passport. Without him, there was only a future of dead dog and virtual penury. As a foreigner, she probably didn't even qualify for a basic pension, might even be deported. Silverburger might have afforded her some protection. He was the sort of person who could.

"There has been no Silverburger movie since *The Coffee Grinders*?"

"No," she admitted.

"And that, forgive me, is quite a long time ago."

"Maybe. Maybe not." This response made no sense.

"Your friend Mr. Silverburger was a one-film producer; a single-movie director."

She sighed. "Yes. But as you say, it is 'an overcrowded profession.' Many people make movies, but usually they have friends with good contacts or with money. Irving was a stranger, a foreigner. He did not have friends with money and connections."

"Until the Pontis. They were foreigners as well."

"This is true," she said. "But is it, as you would say, 'relevant'?" She rolled the word around her Romanian tongue, accentuating the opening *R* and making the word sound surprisingly sexy.

"And you hadn't made a movie since *The Coffee Grinders?*"

"This is also true," she said. "But I have been very busy. With this, with that, as you say in England. Also, as you say, I have been 'resting.' Resting is very important in your country. Everyone in England must rest."

"Not any longer," said Bognor. "That went out with Mrs. Thatcher. Before her, we used to rest a lot. It was considered rather fashionable. But not anymore. We don't rest the way we used to. The only people in the West who understand the idea are the Irish and the Spaniards. Maybe the Italians."

"The Pontis," Ingrid said with feeling, "do not rest. They never rest. They are always working. Even when they seem to be at rest."

Bognor thought of his long liquid lunches with Dibdini at La Locanda Montin and decided it would be best to include at least some Italians in the category of accomplished resters. At least Dibdini got the hang of it. His lunches might not have been free, but at least they were long.

"Maybe Signor Ponti is, as we say 'the exception that proves the rule.' He has money and he works very long hours."

"Yes," she agreed. "Bernardo works and earns the money. Gina does no work and buys many shoes."

Bognor smiled. He had not previously thought of Gina Ponti as Venice's answer to Imelda Marcos.

"Surely, there would have been room for the two of you in a film?" he asked. It seemed a reasonable question, but it led to an angry outburst from Ingrid involving more discordant *poufs*, accompanied by a sort of descant of whimpering from the dog.

"I see," said Bognor. "So you had hostile feelings toward Gina that were both professional and personal."

She nodded vigorously.

"I didn't like her," she said. And Bognor suddenly realized what it must be like to have a rival who was twenty years younger and had a rich husband and as many shoes as she wanted. Ingrid had perfectly good reasons for wanting Gina dead but none, as far as he could see, for wishing the same fate for Irving Silverburger.

He let himself out and saw as he left that the little poodle was baring her yellow teeth at no one in particular while her mistress was helping herself to another hefty Gordon's.

10

"So," said Bognor, "all our people were in Venice at the time of his death; all paid for by him. But none had much of a motive."

Contractor looked thoughtful.

"Motives aren't wet fish," he said. "They don't always slap you in the face. They're not always obvious."

"No, but . . ." said Bognor, knowing that fundamentally he and Contractor agreed. It was deeply mysterious, but there was no reason for the Swanleys, Trevor, or Ingrid Vincent wanting Silverburger dead. Rather the reverse. They all benefited or stood to benefit from his life and increased prosperity. Just the Venetian trip itself. None of them would have had the funds or the inclination to visit La Serenissima without him. Let alone have lunch at Harry's Dolci. On the other hand, you had to ask why exactly Silverburger had asked them there in the first place. Surely, he didn't have a foreboding. He can't have intended the Venetian adventure as a last farewell. Or could he? It was quite odd.

He and his acolyte were having a desultory brainstorming when Minnie came in and said that there was a persistent caller with a funny foreign voice for Sir Simon. She didn't think he was selling double-glazing or tax relief; he sounded as if he was closer than New Delhi and she couldn't get rid of him. Would Sir Simon mind awfully if she put him through? Otherwise, he would be on forever, and she would never get anything done.

It was Bernardo Ponti. He and Gina were just passing through on their way to the country, and they had been talking to Michael Dibdini, who was an old friend and said to give him a call some time and have a chat. He and Gina were at the RAC, but only for a moment as they were off to Kettering on the train any minute, and they'd have a car waiting, but why didn't he come on down for lunch one day. It would be awfully nice to see him and bring his wife, if he felt so inclined. Michael had told them so much about her, but now he must dash or they'd never get to the station in time for the train. So toodle pip, but give us a buzz sometime. We're in the book in Newton under Ponti, and it's not far to Kettering, and we'll make sure you're met, and we'll have you back in two shakes of a duck's whatsit.

And Ponti hung up, leaving Bognor dazed and as speech-less as he had been throughout this breathless monologue, which had been delivered in a style Bognor associated with the younger sons of Indian princes doing geography at Christ Church. No one in real life actually spoke like that. Nor had a place in Northants or dropped the initials of the Royal Auto-mobile Club, which is where Nigel Dempster used to play squash with Jeffrey Archer and is really just a glorified hotel albeit on Pall Mall. Anyone can join.

Contractor looked quizzically, cocking a well-groomed eyebrow but not asking the question outright.

"Ponti," said Bognor, "wanting to say 'hello.' Claimed to be an old mate of Michael's. Which I doubt. And Minnie's right. He talked funny. Not predictable funny, but funny, funny." He liked Minnie. He had rescued her from the typ-ing pool, which was a fate worse than death. He valued her shrewdness, which was quirky but real.

"What do you mean, 'talked funny'?"

"Last person I heard talking like that was someone who called himself the Uvaraj of Thangardrur. Claimed to be studying at Oxford, which I doubt. He sounded like a character out of a P. G. Wodehouse book, only on speed and about to be drowned. Half-drowned perhaps. Not real any-way. Something he'd made up without recourse to the genu-ine article."

"So he's not the genuine article?"

"He's trying to pass himself off as a British country gent. He's not genuine at that, but then who is nowadays? In fact, he seems to be an Italian financier with a much younger wife. I don't see any reason to doubt that."

"So you'll see him here?"

"Wants to give me lunch at his pad in rural Northants."

"And you're going?"

"Why not? I like the idea of Venice cum Pseudley."

"Whereabouts in Northampton?"

"Newton," he said.

"The Rose of the English Shires."

"The what?"

Contractor repeated the phrase. It suggested knowledge but not real knowledge. Contractor had the first in spades; the second came with experience, which was what Bognor liked to believe he had.

"Sounds suspiciously like something dreamed up by the marketing department somewhere," he said. "Anything with rose in it has an unreal, adman's tinge to it. Real people don't do roses."

"Oh," protested Contractor, "that's unfair."

"Who said anything about real life being fair?" said Bognor.

"No, but," said Contractor.

"I know your 'no, buts,'" said Bognor. "I don't trust them. They mean you disagree which elsewhere would be insubordination. And elsewhere has a point. I'm too lenient."

"So you're seeing Mr. and Mrs. Ponti in the country here. Then what?"

"We need to establish why Trevor was in *The Coffee*

Grinders when he said he was back in Riga with an unpro-
nounceable name with an *S* on the end. You'd better do that.
I will see the Pontis, and then it's probably time I saw Father
Carlo and the gondolier and the Russian girl, neither of
whom sound any better than they should be, which doesn't
necessarily make them murderers but definitely makes them
plausible suspects."

"But that means going to Venice?"

"Yes."

"Immediately after a day out in the country."

"Very observant."

"So you spend your time on days out in this country and
jolly jaunts to foreign parts. All at the taxpayers' expense."

It was on the tip of his tongue for Bognor to say that it
was all in the line of duty, but he thought better of it. It was
true up to a point, but only up to a point and his subordinate
knew it. He remembered resenting Parkinson's perks. They
had been relatively few, for Parkinson was a parsimonious
soul not given to pleasure or excess but even so, if there was
anything that seemed even mildly exotic, he snaffled it leaving Bognor to grizzle. At least he would have grizzled if he
felt that he would not, one day, step into Parkinson's shoes
and enjoy what he had. It was a compensation for growing
old and no longer being sound in wind and limb. Age and
experience and wisdom meant chauffeurs and long lunches
and foreign travel. At least it had done so before the forces of
correctness stirred themselves and moved abroad. Nowadays,
the Puritans were in charge. Fun was a forgotten concept and

meritocracy ruled. The compensation was that these things went in cycles as anyone trained, like Bognor, in history knew perfectly well. The tragedy for Simon was that he was in the wrong part of the cycle. When he was junior, the boss had all the enjoyment and when he was senior all pretense of enjoyment had vanished. Contractor, by contrast, was in the right place at the right time and would, in time, enjoy respect, leisure, and perks—all of which Bognor felt he was denied. It was ever thus.

"I thought Dibdini was handling the Italian end," said Contractor.

"Up to a point," said Bognor, using the phrase in its Scoop-Waugh sense to mean a resounding negative expressed with argument-avoiding ambiguity.

"You mean he's not?" Contractor was not dumb.

"I mean what I mean," said Bognor. "I like Michael. He's very good at his job. But at the end of the day, he's foreign." This xenophobia, expressed with all the natural certainty of the British National Party was not intended patronizingly or cynically. Bognor simply believed that the British belief in justice and their system of achieving it was unique and superior. He took little pleasure in this but believed it to be a fact, incapable of serious dispute.

"So he is in charge and yet he's not in charge," said Contractor who, not being of exclusively British descent, was able to see such equivocation for the facile obfuscation that it really was. Bognor, being British, thought it rather sophisticated. "So you have to go and give him a hand and then endorse his findings for home consumption. Bear in mind, that Silverburger was a US citizen murdered on Italian soil, which means that he's none of our business."

"Technically perhaps," Bognor agreed loftily, "but Silverburger was a citizen of the world, so his death is everybody's business, especially SIDBOT's. Besides, he spent a lot of time here, and he could have been knocked off by a British passport holder. More important, I make the rules around here and if I say his murder comes within my jurisdiction, come within my jurisdiction it most certainly does."

"That's making the rules up as you go along," said Contractor.

"Yes."

Contractor sighed. "Just so long as we agree about something," he said.

Bognor said nothing, which could be construed as a response to this, but asked Contractor, not for the first time in this or other investigations, whether he had any solutions to offer.

"On balance, Boss," he said, "I agree with you."

Bognor said that was just as well, but he wondered if Contractor had any bright ideas. He usually did at this stage of the proceedings, particularly when Bognor was unsure of himself as he so often was.

"I don't believe the murderer was any of the people to whom you've talked so far," he ventured. He was evidently thinking out loud, which was one of his more attractive attributes.

"Does that include the Pontis?"

"Not really," said Contractor, "because you haven't spoken to them properly. Just on the phone. I don't think that counts. You have to be there in person. It has to be a proper interview."

"So the telephone doesn't count. In fact, electronics are so susceptible to security risk and to tampering that nothing really counts if it's done on the Internet, even if it's hedged around with the most abstruse security precautions."

"Security precautions can't compete with any known electronics," said Contractor.

Bognor smiled and nodded. "Which is why we rely on such apparently old-fashioned methods," he said. "The tried and tested are invaluable simply because they are tried and tested. If it ain't broke, it don't need fixing. Or words to that effect. It's another way of saying that old-fashioned interrogation remains the best way of getting at the truth."

"Does that include torture?"

Bognor scowled. "You know perfectly well it doesn't include torture," he said. "Only villainous idiots such as George Bush, Cheney, and Rumsfeld believe in torture. Torture is morally indefensible, contrary to the Geneva Convention and practically useless."

"But if it were practically useful, you'd ignore the first two considerations?"

"I didn't say that."

"You implied it."

"No," said Bognor. "You inferred it. That's not the same."

"Now we're dealing in semantics," said Contractor. "Nitpicking. I don't believe you think any of the people to whom you have spoken face to face in connection with the Silverburger murder actually killed him. That isn't the same as saying they didn't; much less that no one on either the English or the Italian list were responsible. But I sense that is what you're beginning to believe. It's not clear-cut, and you're wondering if the killing wasn't random."

"Speculation," said Bognor.

"Did you know that there are people in the counterespionage world who believe you can explain things in terms of multiple choice?"

"You mean Professor Plum did it with (a) the spanner, (b) the dagger, (c) the revolver, or (d) the lead piping in (a) the conservatory, (b) the library, (c) the pantry, or (d) the bathroom?"

"I'm a great believer in the lead piping in the library when all else fails," said Contractor. "But I can believe it. Death reduced to board game. But then you could say that life is just an animated board game, a sort of Snakes and Ladders with knobs on."

"You could say that," agreed Bognor, "and there are those who do. For me, however, lunch in the Rose of the English Shires beckons. Could you see about the times of the trains to Kettering and back and let me know ASAP?"

The Kettering train was fast, and he was in the Northampton countryside well before lunch. Chauffeured car and prepaid first-class tickets meant that it cost him nothing, and he traveled with only the morning's paper and his thoughts for company. The paper was full of nothing as usual, and he was far better informed than any of its reporters or editors thanks to his own research and to a careful study of the Internet. Time was when this would not have been the case and a studious perusal of the morning's press would have been essential for both professional and social reasons. Sadly, this was no longer the case. He was constantly being told both in public and private that the days of the old-fashioned newspapers were numbered and that print was doomed. If this were true, he believed that the papers and their greedy proprietors had only themselves to blame. Newsgathering was a sophisticated, time-consuming, and costly business. The minute you lost sight of that and tried to make money from "news," you and traditional papers were in ruins. QED; fact of life; sad but true.

England slipped by like speeded up film; a blur of images, celluloid in their unreality. He sat in first class, insulated from the polloi back in steerage, insulated from the world outside, insulated from everything. This was life in the fast lane; the life of a successful man, one who had made something of his life in the western world far removed from smelly socks, from toil, from horny-handed anything at all. This was how the other half lived, except that it wasn't the half of it. This was how a miniscule proportion of haves lived, at the expense of the have-nots. The great unwashed were condemned to a life in steerage; the very few were in the Queen's Grill eating caviar, drinking Krug, and waiting for icebergs.

He was reflecting on this when the train pulled into

Kettering, once the capital of a thriving boot-and-shoe industry; now the main town in nothing very much. Kettering was the hub of various Roses of the Shires, once significant and thriving, now depressed if not quite as derelict as Detroit.

The car was waiting by the main exit: standard issue cab with driver in sheepskin coat, driving gloves, and standard patter about those he had had in the back of his vehicle. Bognor sat in the front, a democratic habit he and Monica had acquired in the Antipodes, and asked the driver if he was busy. The cabbie, mildly irked at having to remove a half-eaten KIT KAT and a half-perused girlie magazine from the front seat, said not very on account of the depression, but he supposed he shouldn't grumble, and the two lapsed into silence as more of picture postcard passed in a synthetic glaze before Bognor's eyes. More slowly than on the train, but otherwise much the same.

Newton may or may not have been the Rose of the Shires, but it was pretty in a pretty way. Some villages boasted the sort of inhabitants who would and could join together to secure an increased speed of broadband. Newton was such a village. The houses were beautifully kept, lovely to look at, and did not look as if they were much lived in. They certainly weren't frayed at the edges.

Ponti obviously heard the cab on the gravel of his drive for he opened the door just before Bognor got out. He was wearing tweed, naturally. It was obviously his idea of what the English gentleman wore in the country, but it was not only, like his house, insufficiently frayed around the edges to be a real gentleman's suit, it also had a red thread in its pattern, which was, Bognor thought, a dead giveaway.

"Welcome to Newton in the Willows," said his host, giving the village its tourist board name. He smelled of aftershave, another telltale factor. An Englishman would have reeked of BO. A black Labrador came out and sniffed at Bognor's fly. Like its master, it was too well groomed. It answered to the name Dog, which Bognor thought surprisingly good. "Next time, you must leave time for a walk. There's a good one from the Eleanor Cross in Geddington. J. L. Carr was keen on Eleanor Crosses. He saved Saint Faith's, the church. He has passed away, sadly, but his biographer lives somewhere close by. He is a butcher, I believe."

Bognor thought he'd got his wires crossed about butchery and Byron Rogers, and a real Englishman would never have described death as "passing away," but in other respects, he was pretty near right. Bognor awarded him a mental seven out of ten and allowed him to be motioned inside.

The house was eerily impersonal yet not like a hotel. Bognor tried to put his finger on it and came up with frayed edges once more. There were none.

Mrs. Ponti, aka Gina, was waiting in the drawing room. *Lamb dressed,* he thought, thinking of her more mature rival in Kingston, *as lamb.* She was much younger than her husband; looked it, dressed like it, and arguably behaved like it. She reminded Bognor of the Italian girl who married the French president; at one and the same time mildly overawed and slightly bored. A difficult combination to pull off, particularly on purpose.

"Sir Simon," she said, holding out a hand, attached to a jangling arm. Bognor kissed it, which he suspected was the correct thing to do but not what one did in Northamptonshire. Such behavior would have been thought effeminate, and he was glad there was no one except Signor Ponti to see.

"Jolly nice of you to ask me down," he said.

She didn't say anything but merely simpered.

"Jolly nice part of the world," he said, "though I'm afraid I don't know it awfully well. Friends of mine used to shoot at Broughton House and Rockingham but not me, alas."

The first half of this was a lie; the second all too true. It was what chaps said and did in this part of the world, though not the Pontis and their friend Silverburger. Bognor felt snobbish even as he said it, and also a bit of a parvenu. He knew he could not have got away with it with people who really knew what was what. He wondered if the Pontis fitted in to Venetian society and whether they would seem at home in some sort of sepulchral palazzo riddled with damp and decay. He thought probably not. Too much money. Too much effort. Bernardo, in particular, tried too hard.

The prints were either David Gentleman or school of. The china came from a smart antique shop. Everything gave the impression of being put together rapidly and at some expense. Lunch, which was served presently, was dished up by a manservant in striped trousers and a crisp jacket who knew how to do clever things with dessert spoons and held one hand behind his back while serving. The food, some sort of vegetable soup and some sort of chicken with rice, was too good but above all too recognizable. Likewise the wine, which was a presentable Orvieto and a passable Barolo. Italian and much too good for the average deputy lieutenant who would have served plonk or pale ale and food that could have been fish or fowl and might have been either, disguised as it would have been in a tepid and tasteless sauce.

"Did you know Irving Silverburger well?" inquired Bognor when rent-a-butler had gone.

"Alas, poor Irving," exclaimed his host, pouring more wine into a cut-glass goblet and looking lachrymose. "But what a stylish way to leave. Like something from one of his own movies."

Bognor thought of saying something along the lines of *The Coffee Grinders* being one of the worst films he had ever seen and couldn't remember a single memorable death other than the bloke who was scalded to death by a Gaggia machine, but he decided not to. Instead, he said, "Shot in the back by someone during Carnival," which everyone knew and was banal to the point of being quite stupid.

"Someone armed with a crossbow," said Gina, "which means he probably wasn't English. Didn't the English always use the longbow? Hearts of oak."

"It could have been a woman," said Bernardo. "There is no strength involved in the crossbow. At Crécy, the bowmen of England were big fellows, like bouncers. They had biceps because you needed them to pull the string properly. But anyone can use a crossbow. It requires skill but not strength."

"Do you think the assassin was a woman?"

Bernardo slurped from the side of the spoon nearest him—another gastronomic solecism that would not have gone unnoticed in proper, snobbish society. It wouldn't have passed muster at the Bullingdon. Boris Johnson and David Cameron wouldn't have approved.

"I don't think about the gender of the person who killed him, but nevertheless the killing had something beautiful. Did not your Mr. Yeats write about a fearful symmetry?"

"He wasn't one of ours, actually," said Bognor. "He was Irish. And anyway, it was William Blake. Writing about tigers. 'Tyger! Tyger! burning bright.' Only, for some reason I can't remember, he spelled it with a *Y* not an *I*. Still, he *was* one of ours." He drank some soup without making any noise.

They were looking at him suspiciously. Policemen weren't supposed to know things such as that. Nor to drink their soup noiselessly. Bognor was not, he kept telling himself, that sort of policeman. But they didn't know that. Not yet anyway. And anyway they were foreign. Even more reason for not knowing.

"I'm sorry," said Bognor, not in the least sorry but saying that he was because it was what a certain sort of Englishman said at the beginning of a sentence when he was attempting to wrest the conversation back to its beginnings. "You were telling me how well you knew Irving."

"We met in Davos," said Bernardo, "some years ago.

BG." He laughed. "I, too, am sorry. BG is a family code for Before Gina. We have been together for three years now, and Davos was before that. So, yes, I had known Irving a long time. Gina, less long."

"So really he was your friend rather than Mrs. Ponti's."

Gina, who had no more idea of the English way with soup than her husband, demurred.

"Irving was *our* friend," she said. "To begin, he was Bernardo's friend, but since the last year or so, he was a friend of the both of us."

She smiled and must have depressed a hidden bell push in the best country tradition because the hired man shimmered in and cleared away, reappearing as noiselessly with the chicken and rice.

"I see," Bognor said after the three of them had been served and were alone once more. He didn't, of course, and he was at a loss about Davos. There was some sort of pseudo-geo-economic conference there every year, but neither Bernardo nor certainly Silverburger had that sort of financial clout. He supposed they might have been there as some sort of hangers-on, but it seemed more likely that they had simply been skiing or après-skiing or whatever one did in the snowy mountains in Switzerland in winter. Bognor had never understood the point, much preferring heat.

"Such a shame that at the end of the day, of his day, that *The Coffee Grinders* was his only film," said Bognor. "It will become a sort of last will and testament, a celluloid memorial." He sighed. "Alas, poor Irving."

"In a way, yes," said Bernardo, shoveling chicken and rice into his mouth with the fork turned up like a spoon. "But out of defeat we hope to grab a little victory. Isn't that so, my dear?"

He smiled adoringly and proprietorially at his wife who smiled back though not in as wholehearted a way as her husband and in a way that made Bognor's antennae sing.

"That you should have been a star was what Irving would have wished. And our money will make his wish come true. Isn't that a fact?"

To which, she simpered some more, and Bognor felt sure at once that she had married Mr. Ponti for his money and for his power and influence. Without him, she would never have been a film star.

Bernardo raised his glass.

"I drink to the memory of a great man," he said, "to a great man of the movies. And I drink also to the success of his final memorial. Lady and Gentleman, I give you *The Lemon Peelers*."

There was no doubt about the Pontis' intentions. He was going to use his money to produce the film that Irving G. Silverburger wanted to make, and his wife, Gina, was to play the leading role. That was their wish, and they canonized it by making it also the last testament of Irving G. Silverburger. It had been the final wish of their friend, and in carrying out their own wish, they were also executing his. They only had the Pontis' word for this, but who was going to argue with them?

"How interesting," said Bognor, who was certainly not about to pick a fight. He cut a piece of chicken, which was good, and, he guessed, organic-ish and local. It probably came from a nearby barn. Butchered perhaps by Byron Rogers. He allowed himself the ghost of a smile and settled back for their version of the plot so far.

"We'd discussed it with Irving before . . ." began Bernardo.

"He was killed," said Gina. She suffered from no visible qualms when it came to discussing the murder of their friend. Unlike her husband, who obviously believed that there were proprieties to be observed. "There's no point beating about the bushes. He was murdered."

Bognor ignored this, politely, enjoying the lunch and smiling serenely.

"So," he said, "what's the plot? Roughly."

"Well," Bernardo thought hard. "We thought we would open in the local village shop."

"There is no shop," said Gina. "We would have to make believe."

"Quite." Bognor smiled encouragingly. "So you have a village shop, fabricated, but in a rural English village not a million miles from the Rose Queen of the Shires."

"Exactly," said Bernardo. "You have hit the screw on the top."

"Nail on the head," Bognor said pleasantly.

Both Pontis seemed surprised by this rejoinder.

"Gina enters the shop, and she asks the person who is serving from behind the counter if she may please have a lemon. And this person is saying that they do not carry exotic fruit."

Gina herself took up the story, "Because the counter-jumper, she says there is no call for exotic fruit such as the lemon. And then there is a cut to me behind a bar somewhere, and I am peeling a lemon to put in the dry martini, which is shaken but not stirred."

"*À la mode de Bond,*" explained Bernardo.

"Actually," said Bognor, "Bond preferred an olive and later switched to vodka. And when he was asked if he preferred his drink shaken or stirred, he asked, 'Do I look like I give a damn?' That was in *Casino Royale.* Ian Fleming wasn't nearly as good a writer as his brother Peter. Better known though. And more of a drinker. They reduced the strength of Gordon's so you're better off with Tanqueray. Personally, I prefer Plymouth."

And he took another mouthful of the chicken, followed by a swig of Barolo. He would have been just as happy with a Barbera, but he had a quaffer's taste and a slight aversion to the Nebbiolo grape. However, he judged, correctly, that his erudition on the subject of lemon in a dry martini was enough showing off for one meal.

The Pontis were impressed but not overly so. They obviously thought he was bluffing but did not know enough to call it.

"We would like it to be a suitable memorial to a dear friend," said Bernardo. "He would have wished it."

"A pity it couldn't have been made while he was alive," said Bognor.

"I agree," said Bernardo. "His death was very shocking. However, he talked of his plans in great detail, and we know what he would have wished."

"Good," said Bognor. "What about the lunch at Harry's Dolci?"

"The lunch at Harry's Dolci?" they asked together.

"Yes," said Bognor. Forget hell being other people, his idea of the inferno was asking a question that was batted back as an uncomprehending repetition until the end of time.

"The lunch at Harry's Dolci," he repeated inanely, fully expecting the words to come boomeranging back like some maddening echo. He was surprised, therefore, and mildly relieved to hear Bernardo reply in immaculate foreigner's English.

"It was very agreeable."

"And Irving paid?"

The pause was one of embarrassment. Both Pontis stared at the ground.

Eventually, Bernardo said, "Nobody paid."

Bognor who had been brought up in an old-fashioned world in which everyone paid more or less immediately and credit was relatively unknown (unless one had an account at somewhere such as Harrods in which case payment was vulgar) looked surprised. "But someone must have paid."

There was another silence, punctuated only by chewing and slurping.

Eventually, Bernardo said, "Nobody paid. Irving had one of those pink plastic cards, and he waved it at everyone and smiled. He was very charming. He seldom paid. Other people usually paid. Or someone. He usually managed, as you would say in your country, 'to get away with it.'"

"I see," said Bognor, seeing nothing and understanding less. He supposed charm would get you everywhere, especially if you were Italian. Well, American Italian of Jewish inclination. Actually, Silverburger was an all-American mongrel. That was the point, if indeed he had one. "Bit of a sponger." It was what men of his generation thought about those who were always on the take. Silverburger was strong on the take, but he did not seem to have a lot of give.

"I wouldn't say that," said Gina, managing to seem almost thoughtful to one who believed she had that capacity. Bognor was not of their number. He didn't believe Gina was a thinker, and he didn't believe this was just a matter of inclination. He did not believe that she had that capacity even if she had wished to think. Which, on the whole, she didn't. Vapidity suited her, and even though she had no ability to be anything else, she was happy enough to have nothing but good looks between the ears.

"Then what exactly would you say?" asked Bognor, pretending that she might have something to say that would be of interest.

Bernardo, who had a brain, came to the rescue.

"I think what Gina means," he began in the traditional disclaimer of the defensive partner, "is that Irving had *real* charm. With some people, it's just skin deep, but Irving wasn't like that. His charm ran deep. He was marked indelibly, through and through, like a stick of rock."

"Blackpool," Bognor said fatuously. It was a matter of word association. Force of habit acquired by living with a crossword fiend. It was vicarious response, but it elicited a joint rejoinder of "*Che?*" which reminded him that he was dealing with people whose first language was not English.

"The most famous candy of that kind comes from Blackpool. When you say that Irving Silverburger's charm was like something printed on a stick of rock, I'm afraid the average Englishman thinks of Blackpool. Though there's little charming about Blackpool. If you see what I mean."

Neither Ponti gave the slightest sign of seeing what he meant, and Bognor wasn't entirely sure what he meant himself. He knew, however, that he should stop digging and change the subject.

"The projected movie," he said, finishing his food and setting the knife and fork in a neat parallel just as he had been taught in school, "is a sort of homage to Irving Silverburger. But how much of Silverburger will it contain? Did he leave much? Will it be slavish? Or free? What kind of adaptation do you plan? If you intend an adaptation. After all, they do say that imitation is the sincerest form of flattery. Will it be a sort of ersatz Silverburger? Hamlet without the ghost? A Silverburger movie with no Silverburger?"

He looked at the Pontis in a polite conversational way as if he were simply the perfect guest and not an importunate pretend-policeman. After all, he was only returning their chat to the starting point.

"What happens," he asked, "after the shop?"

"Sex," said Gina. "We have to have sex. It is essential."

"All Irving's films," said her husband, a little more decorously, "have men and women. The men and women have . . . relations. It is natural."

"Essential," said Gina. "It is essential."

"So it's a sort of soft-porn Aga-saga in the style of Silverburger?"

"Not soft porn," the husband said with the vehemence of one who has been rightly accused. "Very tasteful. The taste is essential. Irving was always in the best possible taste."

"Exactly," said Mrs. Ponti. "Taste is of the essence."

Whether or not Irving G. Silverburger was into taste or had the first idea what it meant was debatable. Indeed, Bognor would like to have seen the matter debated, but he felt that this was not the place. A pity.

"Of course," said Bognor. "Lots of violins. Good photography. Like an advertisement for bread. Or the tourist board."

He hadn't meant to sound patronizing and went slightly pink when he realized the effect he had had.

Nothing, however, was said.

"So," he said, puncturing the silence, which was a little awkward, "when do you go into production?"

Technical term. The plates were cleared. Pudding was summer. It was pink; there was cream. That, like the chicken, was probably local, unlike the fruit, which had been frozen, and the bread, which was factory-sliced and came, he suspected, from a cellophane packet. Perfectly all right, though.

"Production?" asked *la signora*, seeming not to have heard the word before.

"Production," said her husband, almost saving the situation. "We don't have a date yet."

No money, thought Bognor, but he said nothing. He wondered if the film would ever be made or would remain hanging in the air, a suitable subject for conversation and even the occasional lunch. He had spent much of his life avoiding line-shooters who would waste his time and eat his food while discussing a project that everyone knew would never see the light of day. He suspected this was one such.

"No date?" he repeated, spearing a blackberry. "Ah."

"We need to plan properly," explained Ponti. "It's not something you want to ad-lib. I prefer not to fly by the seat of my pants."

"Quite," said Bognor. "On the other hand, you need to preserve spontaneity."

"Absolutely," said his host. "Spontaneity together with meticulous planning. Difficult but the goal to which we must aspire."

"Quite," said Bognor. "And dosh."

"Dosh?" they both said, and Bognor remembered that they were foreign. He finished his summer pudding, and licked his lips.

"Money," he said. "Lucre. Spondulicks. Stuff that makes the world go round."

He wondered if this were right. He had never had a lot himself, and his world revolved in a more or less acceptable fashion. Silverburger had always been short of a few bob, but it didn't seem to have greatly affected his modus operandi. The Pontis were in much the same sort of boat moneywise. As far as their world revolving went, he wasn't entirely sure. Maybe time would tell. He accepted the offer of coffee and watched the back of his hostess as she left for the kitchen and the coffeepot. Nice bottom.

"She will be an adornment," said her husband, catching his guest's mood and gaze.

"Undoubtedly," said Bognor, half-remembering a piece of doggerel by someone such as James Thurber or Ogden Nash about advancing and retreating, "but you still need money."

"Aye," Signor Ponti said unexpectedly, "there's the rub."

"Absolutely," he concurred as *la signora* entered with a tray on which there were three dinky Illy coffee cups, sugar, milk, and a *caffetiera*. The distaff side of the Ponti couple looked even better from the front. Advancing. Bognor thought the verse had something to do with "my sweet sweeting," but he couldn't remember. A proper English couple would have served instant muck in mugs. This was better but lacked authenticity.

She tilted the *caffetiera* and poured. Bognor took his black without sugar. He sipped. It was good and all the better for being foreign.

"My experience," he said, "is that money will buy anything. Even death."

"Meaning?" asked Ponti who may not have been English but was far from stupid.

"Meaning," said Bognor, "exactly what I say. Money will buy death. It could well be that Silverburger was shot by a hired assassin. In which case, the actual killer lacked a real motive. The culpability lies with whoever signed the check."

He smiled. "They say that money is the root of all evil," he said.

The Pontis looked blank. He sighed and sipped. They were about money; that was certain. He wasn't so sure about the evil. The potential was there, the incentive dubious.

He smiled.

They smiled back.

Stalemate.

11

Bognor took the train back from Kettering. Trains were not what they once were. He was a steam *Lady Vanishes* sort of man. He liked Indian railways because they used elderly coal-burning locomotives made in England back when that phase was a guarantee of quality rather than a promise of built-in obsolescence or even imminent disintegration. Nowadays, trains looked more streamlined but did not travel any more speedily. They had evolved a language all of their own so that *passengers* had become *customers*; stations, station stops; and *platform* was a verb. Only the leaves were always the wrong sort. The days of pedestrian descriptive names were long vanished, Beechingized in some modernist purge so that the Somerset and Dorset, aka the Slow and Dirty, had not only vanished, but even if it were still around, would have acquired a mad new name such as Arrival or even Departure. Bognor looked out of the window and tried to think of suitable modern names for the Slow and Dirty.

He failed and snoozed most of the way to London, where he took a cab to the office in order to touch base before returning to his wife's welcome smile. Base was alive and well, and working on as was its wont, well after the call of duty and normal office hours. Base was, of course, Harvey Contractor.

"Hi, Boss," he said, fawning. "Your confessor phoned."

Bognor frowned. He didn't know what he was talking about. Contractor knew perfectly well that his boss was a cheerful agnostic masquerading under the catchall euphemism of the Church of England.

"Said he was staying with his friends at Farm Street. The Jesuits. But he was going to be out to dinner. Sounded as if he did a lot of dinner. And lunch. In fact an all-day-breakfast sort of priest. Sounded foreign. Said his name was Carlo. He rolled the *R*."

"Padre Carlo," said Bognor.

Harvey Contractor gave him an old-fashioned look but said nothing.

"So what brings him to London?"

"*Cherchez le garçon*," Contractor said knowingly.

"That's not fair," said Bognor. "Some of my best Catholic friends are heterosexual. Celibate even."

His subordinate smiled as if he were the only one with all the answers.

"That's not what I hear," he said. "Anyone would think you believe what you read in the papers. You're not the only person with Catholic friends. Most of the men I know were abused at school."

"Don't be silly. Most of the world's Scoutmasters are homosexual. All of us could make a case for having been abused. It's become a sort of Vatican cliché. What did the padre say?"

"Just his name," said Contractor. "Seemed to think it would work miracles. I'd say he was right."

"I'll call Farm Street from home," said Bognor, sweeping his stuff into a brown leather brief case with gold initials, almost illegible from age and use.

He did, too. He and Monica ate underdone steak with a bottle of acceptable Beaujolais and then armed with a glass of Mr. Hine's best cognac, he called the Jesuits and was put through to the Italian guest who had just returned from dining at the hotel across the road. The Connaught, actually. It later transpired that he had been taken as a treat but sent the wine back on the grounds that it was corked. He went to that sort of hostelry frequently. He was that sort of priest.

"Come round for a snifter," he said. "Bring the wife. Lady Bognor."

Bognor was fed up with imitation English gentlemen, and Padre Carlo was clearly just such an item albeit in priest's clothing.

"Actually, I'm a bit tied up," he said, sipping brandy and

smiling indulgently at Lady B. who looked suspiciously at him. She drank a little and rolled her eyes.

He listened for a while as the priest said that he was returning to Italy and had to be at Heathrow by noon. Bognor, naturally, suggested breakfast and found himself being thanked while he agreed meekly to a rendezvous at The Connaught. The office would pay. Even so the priest had an irreligious nerve.

"I take it I'm not included. Also if you end up paying, I will be cross. Very."

Monica treated him like an infant, which he resented but was reluctant to change. A dislike of trivial matters, even when misconceived, allowed him more latitude in matters of importance. That, at least, was his theory.

And so it was that Sir Simon Bognor found himself eating croissants, smoked salmon, and scrambled eggs, accompanied by freshly squeezed orange juice and strong black coffee, while his guest had two soft-boiled eggs and toast. The Connaught was full of suits and enormous hair. The big hair belonged to the fair sex. Many of the suits had none at all. Padre Carlo claimed to have come in order to preach and see a particular confidant. Actually, his main purpose was to purchase some of his trademark monogrammed chocolate and cerise socks from his favorite *chaussettier* in the Burlington Arcade. However, he thought it more tactful to stick to the sermon story. Bognor might have thought the socks extravagant, even foppish, particularly for a Franciscan.

"So," said Simon, "what was your text?"

Padre Carlo was momentarily discomfited but then remembered his sermon.

"Revelation," he said, "with a nod toward W. B. Yeats. Rough beasts. Jerusalem." He dipped some toast into his egg yolk. Despite the socks, he spoke excellent English.

"Slouching," said Bognor, not wishing to be thought ill-read, particularly by a foreigner. "Yeats's beast slouches. As I recall, the one in Revelation did a lot of falling over. Six hundred three score and six. But there were four beasts weren't there? I confess I always found Revelation confusing."

The egg was moist and buttery, just as he liked it. The salmon was wild. Thank God the office would pay.

"Many people find Revelation confusing," conceded Padre Carlo, "though in some ways, it is the most straightforward book in the entire Bible."

"Not for me I'm afraid," said Bognor. "But then I'm afraid I'm a bit of a lukewarm agnostic. If I were the Lord God, I'd spew me out."

He grinned. Padre Carlo seemed unamused.

"Your Mr. Silverburger was religious," said the priest.

"He wasn't mine," said Bognor, more crisply than he intended, "and if he was religious, then the pope's my father."

This time, Father Carlo smiled, but it was a winter gesture, without warmth and with the hint of frost to come.

"The pope is everyone's father," he said, offering the observation as a rebuke, though Bognor who had been brought up in a sound middle-of-the-road Church of Englandism felt that he was in the right and knew best.

"In what sense was Silverburger religious?" Bognor asked, ignoring the vexed question of the pope and paternity. He was genuinely interested for Silverburger seemed the most saturnine person he had encountered in a life devoted to confronting bad.

"He was interested in making a film based on the Bible. He, too, was interested in Revelation, as it happens. Interested in substituting the elders with maidens of some kind; younger than the originals and wearing fewer clothes. He assured me that such things were necessary to secure money. He also said that elderly gentlemen would not be box office. I was to be called the technical adviser, and we expected to fight, but that is inevitable. We would always be friendly and constructive. Also I understood, as you Anglo-Saxons say, 'where he was coming from.' I am a man of the world. Franciscans are nearly all men of the world. That is part of what makes us the people we are."

Bognor thought of the socks but did not mention them. Nor did he allude to the fact that, like the late Irving, he batted and bowled. He did both with a verve and enthusiasm that was infectious but not clerical. Austerity was not his thing. He had a voluptuary's lips and a complexion to match. He suspected the pigmentation of his hair and even its heaviness was not entirely natural. If it were a rug, it was an expensive rug. He also seemed disturbingly at ease in these surroundings, but he would doubtless have said that this was simply being Franciscan.

"And did the Pontis . . . that is to say, were the Pontis involved in these plans?"

"The money was important." The padre had finished his eggs and looked as if he might order more. He contented himself with butter and marmalade on toast. "Mammon had to be placated."

"Quite," said Bognor. "You say that Mr. Silverburger was a religious man."

"Oh yes," said Padre Carlo. "Very definitely so. Not, perhaps, in a conventional way but very religious. Definitely."

"I don't associate him with the Church," said Bognor, "and *The Coffee Grinders* seemed to be a glorification of material things, especially sex."

"Ah, sex," the padre said, as if that explained everything.

"Well, yes," said Bognor. "Extramarital hanky-panky. Having it off with all and sundry. Not good. Not good at all."

Father Carlo put the tips of his fingers together and smiled over the top of them at the ruined eggs, now all shell and no substance.

"Sometimes, I believe that you puritans are only interested in the exchange of bodily fluids."

It was on the tip of Bognor's tongue to protest that he was not in the least puritanical. He thought better of it, however.

"Other sins are more sinful," said Father Carlo. "Killing people is very bad." He looked at the remains of breakfast. "Gluttony also. Very bad. Sex not so bad. If other people are hurt, then not so good, but if not then . . ." He paused, smiled almost with humor. Bognor wouldn't have put it past him to light a cheroot or one of those foul-smelling loose-packed Nazionali cigarettes.

"Killing someone with a crossbow during the Venetian Carnival?" said Bognor.

"Bad," said Padre Carlo. "Very bad indeed. Much worse than an orgasm with someone. Nothing to compare."

"I suppose not," said Bognor.

"The chief of police in Venice says you are in charge," said the Franciscan.

"Very flattering," he said, vowing privately to have more than a word with his Italian friend, "but not accurate. The murder took place on Italian soil so it's in Italian jurisdiction."

"Waters," said Father Carlo. He was nitpicking. "Our friend was shot in a vessel."

"Any idea who did it?"

The priest looked reflective.

"He came to see me in the church. I heard his confession, but I am not, of course, at liberty to tell you what he said."

"Did what he said have any bearing on his death?"

"Alas, I am not able to say. I am bound by my promises."

Bognor did not think Father Carlo was bound by anything. He struck Bognor as being amoral at best and venal at worst, probably both. He had conned breakfast out of SIDBOT and teased its boss. Not cricket.

"Who do you think did it?" Bognor was not given to the full frontal direct approach, preferring something more oblique. In this, he was British in an old-fashioned way—all nudges and winks.

"You are the detective," Father Carlo said with a shrug. "I am just a priest. I am not a solver of murder mysteries. However, I believe the late Mr. Silverburger was a good Christian in his way."

Bognor didn't agree about this, but then he had decided some time ago that the Holy Father was not a particularly good Christian, either.

He asked for the bill. This was substantial, but he paid in cash and added a large tip. Father Carlo thanked him. Bognor nodded.

Both men had coats, duly delivered but requiring more tips. It had been an expensive breakfast. Outside, Bognor's car was waiting. He would sit in the back and read papers while reflecting on a waste of time and of money. He offered Father Carlo a lift, but the man of God said that he would use his own legs and feet, which was not a particular hardship as Farm Street and his guest quarters and bags were only on the other side of the road. Bognor told himself that he must not allow personal dislike to interfere with his professional judgment. Just because he found the Italian loathsome didn't make him a murderer. Possibly the reverse. Many of the murderers Bogor had known were personally quite attractive, the sort of people one would have to dinner. People one wouldn't let near the house were often entirely innocent of serious crime despite their obvious shortcomings as human beings.

"Oh well," Bognor said fatuously, looking back on the extravagant waste of the early hours of the morning, "onward and upward."

The priest suddenly looked gray and deflated. They shook hands and Bognor got into his limo.

Father Carlo waved a sad farewell.

"Very sad and very difficult to lose a brother," he said as the driver eased the car into the rush-hour traffic, leaving Bognor to reflect on what could have been the most revealing sentence of the entire chat and possibly the entire investigation. He wished that his guest had uttered it earlier, wanted to ask him to elaborate, but saw only his retreat toward his temporary home. Slouching, like a strange beast. Perhaps, however, he had been granted a blinding flash of revelation. A question for Contractor.

12

Contractor thought it was just a turn of phrase. He obviously considered his boss wet behind the ears and not with water from Jordan.

"It's the sort of thing god-botherers say," he said. He himself was an agnostic or non-practicing Muslim so he disliked Christians, especially Roman Catholics. "He's a man of the cloth. And Italian. Naturally, he thinks all men are brothers. He's amazingly wrong, but there you go. Nothing in it."

"I'm not so sure," said Bognor. "I think he was claiming consanguineous fraternity."

"Long words and concepts will get you nowhere at all," said the overbright minion.

"Check him out anyway," said Bognor, "and that's an order."

Giving instructions such as this always made him feel good. He was used to discussion, disagreement, debate. Insolence was acceptable in his opinion if it were dumb. Being able to indulge himself thus was almost the only perk of nearing retirement.

The bad news was that his wife agreed with the staff. In other words, Monica, Lady Bognor, thought the same as Harvey Contractor. To make matters worse, Monica specialized in insolence, but she didn't do dumb.

"Figure of speech," she said. "At least that depends on the state of one's belief. It's the sort of thing you'd expect a Catholic priest to say."

The skepticism was almost tangible. Just as well, he thought, that they were talking on the telephone and not face-to-face in the same room.

"I don't think he was talking figuratively," he said. "He doesn't strike me as a figurative sort of person."

"Well," she said, "you should know."

"What's that supposed to mean?" He had little or no idea, but he was aware that they were having a row and that it had something to do with the fact that he had been having an expensive breakfast with a priest who claimed to be related to the deceased. Monica obviously thought she should have been enjoying the expensive breakfast.

"It just means that priests think everyone is their brother or sister. They go about the place making the sign of the cross and blessing everyone in sight. They don't necessarily believe a word of it. In fact, many of them think it's the mumbo-jumbo it so obviously is."

"You go to church often enough," he protested.

"Because I like the noise. That doesn't mean I believe the nonsense. The idea that the devil has all the best tunes is rubbish in a literal sense. God has some very merry numbers, and his servants have a good line in frocks. But that doesn't make them serious or believable."

"You could have fooled me."

"Not difficult. You're one of the most gullible men I know."

This wasn't true. It was a typical calumny. Bognor believed that in a number of important respects he was a figment of his wife's imagination. Her image of him bore little or no relation to reality. The trouble was that she was so forceful, people were inclined to believe her. And the more he grinned and bore it, the more they believed her.

"I just wonder if he was really related to Silverburger," said Bognor. "I mean, in a way, with which we all agree and sympathize. In the sight of man rather than the sight of God."

"A real follower of the rule of Saint Francis isn't much interested in the sight of man. The sight of God is much more important even if it passeth all understanding. Which it does."

"That's not my idea of the average Franciscan," he said. "My experience is that they're much more interested in their fellow man than most contemplatives. They're friars after all. Jolly souls. Convivial. Wasn't Tuck a Franciscan?"

"Friar Tuck was a fictional device. He didn't exist. In any

case, you're thinking of Anglican Franciscans. Not the same thing at all."

"Tuck was pre-Reformation." Bognor had read modern history. He suspected Monica of having acquired her knowledge of the subject from the writings of Sir Arthur Bryant. Like Barbara Cartland. The certainty was certainly similar.

"Would have been if he were real."

At least Lady Bognor was consistent.

"My feeling is that Roman Catholic Franciscan friars can differentiate between generalities about *fraternité, egalité,* and similar revolutionary claptrap and real-life blood brotherhood. And what I'm saying is that Father Carlo admitted to me that he and Irving Silverburger had the same mother and the same father. That's all, but it's interesting. That's all."

Monica said a rude word and put the phone into its cradle. There was a click, then nothing. Bognor found himself staring stupidly at the silent receiver. At length, he replaced the phone and sat staring at it thoughtfully. Then he decided to Skype his old friend and colleague in Venice.

"Michael," he said, smiling. Dibdini had an old machine, which necessitated a headset and microphone. This made him look like an old-fashioned commentator of the Snagge era. He half expected a mellifluous "In . . . out, one . . . out, two . . . out," as if he were describing the Oxford and Cambridge boat race.

After they had exchanged greetings in broken Italanglais, Bognor remarked nonchalantly that he had breakfasted with Father Carlo.

"Ah," said Dibdini, "he is everywhere that Carlo."

"We had breakfast at The Connaught."

"Ah," Dibdini said again, but chuckling this time. "The Board of Trade will have paid for breakfast. Father Carlo never pays for his meals, but he eats very well. One day, I, too, must take a vow of poverty." He smiled. "And did you discover anything? Was it worth the price? Will Her Majesty's Government forgive the extravagance?"

"Perhaps," said Bognor. "Tell me, Michael, do you have friends at the Frari?"

Dibdini gave the impression of considering the question intimately, examined his fingers, and said at length, "But why do you ask?"

It was on the tip of Bognor's tongue to repeat the old saw about never responding to a question with another question, but he thought better of it and merely repeated his sentence.

Once more, Dibdini appeared to think. Eventually, he seemed to come to a decision.

"I have a particular friend who knows about the Franciscans in Venice. He knows many of their secrets, which are numerous. He understands where, as you say, the bodies are buried."

"Might he be able to tell us about Father Carlo?"

Dibdini inspected his fingernails ostentatiously and at length. Eventually, he spoke, "What exactly do you wish to know?"

"I need to know where Father Carlo comes from," said Bognor. "I need to know who his parents were. Whether he has or had brothers and sisters."

Dibdini smiled.

"I see you have heard the rumors," he said.

Bognor said nothing but smiled back, unflinching.

"I will speak to my friend."

Bognor reflected that, while some of his best friends were foreign, foreigners, even when friendly, were not the same as the British. They were, well, foreign, even when much nicer than most British people. Dibdini was a case in point. Bognor was very fond of him, regarded him as a friend, thought him much nicer than the average Brit and certainly much nicer than anyone in the prime minister's office even though they were nearly all British. Having said all that, Dibdini was foreign and, as such, unreadable at times. Bognor couldn't always fathom him. This didn't matter, but it could be disconcerting. By the same token, Father Carlo who was much less likable was just as foreign and therefore, in a sense, just as impenetrable.

"How did Accrington Stanley play?" his friend wanted to know. This was further evidence of Michael's foreignness. The only people who supported Accrington Stanley either lived in Accrington or abroad. British football fans just sniggered. This was doubtless unfair on Accrington of which Bognor knew nothing at all apart from the name and that of the football club. If pressed, he would have said that it was full of men in flat caps who ate pies and raced pigeons plus their long-suffering wives who affected shapeless clothes and their children who seldom if ever washed and wore clogs on their feet. And the loos, if they existed, were outdoors. This only showed how little he knew, how prejudiced he was, and how much less open-minded than Dibdini. He hadn't the faintest idea what had happened to Accrington Stanley and cared less. He hated football with a passion and associated it with the above, but above all with money of which he had not nearly enough and not nearly as much as those who played the game professionally, even if they played for a team as poor as Accrington Stanley.

"Sorry," he said. "Haven't the foggiest."

The North-South divide, he reflected, was all too real. He regarded himself as tolerably enlightened, liberal even, and yet he knew that he had little or no understanding of life north of the Trent and didn't much care for the idea of it. He knew that his feelings were reciprocated by the denizens of that baffling part of the world. The really sad thing was that he cared so little. Much the same applied to abroad, and yet he had a sneaking regard for "Johnny Foreigner" particularly now that the Great had been so emphatically removed from Britain and by a member of the Bullingdon no less. The fact that he was from Brasenose went some way to explaining why we now had aircraft carriers with no aircraft, but not far. The French would never have countenanced such a humiliation, or any number of countries on which we had once upon a time looked down our long and aristocratic nose.

Father Carlo was foreign, so was the deceased, so, for that matter, was his partner in crime prevention. Being foreign made them suspicious, almost as much as if they had come from somewhere vague and cold such as the north. Time was when the sort of cut-glass accent to which Bognor aspired, but which had vanished into a new world of glottal stops and adenoidal cat noises made popular by such orally challenged public figures as Prime Minister Edward Heath, was the correct voice of law and order. Nowadays, if someone talked proper with the kind of voice that Bognor still regarded as accentless and "correct," it was a demonstration of guilt. Time was when the good guys had been at English public schools; nowadays, a public education was evidence of nefariousness. Bad guys went to Eton.

He sighed. He hoped prejudice had never colored his forensic judgement. He was, he told himself, completely open and fair, acknowledging no bias toward evil in anybody irrespective of class, creed, or color. He was a believer in science, objectivity, and—above all—fair play. Just because someone was underprivileged, physically threatened, or in some way less than adequate, didn't make them criminal. It helped. He knew that statistics proved unpalatable truths. But he was above such lies. He approached all his cases with an entirely open mind unsullied by anything at all. To him, all men were innocent until proved otherwise. Having said that, he acknowledged that some were less likely to be innocent than others.

Foreigners, he said to himself. He really meant *bloody foreigners* but didn't use the adjective even silently to himself.

"Accrington was one of the founders of the league only it collapsed and was taken over by another club called Stanley

Villa, which played at a ground called Stanley Park or something. They were refounded in the sixties by someone called Stanley Wotherspoon, which was nice. They were recently readmitted to the league at the expense of Oxford, who originally replaced them. They're really bad. Why do you support them?"

"I like the name," said Dibdini. "It is very English. Very curious."

There was no answer to this, and he did not attempt one.

"What rumors about Father Carlo?" he asked instead. "He seems smarmy to me, but that's not a crime. Nor even a sin."

"This," said Dibdini, looking at his fingernails again, "and that."

"I see," said Bognor, seeing nothing. Father Carlo always seemed a bit of a pantomime villain and more panto than villain. Still . . . this was pure prejudice. Bognor disliked unctuousness, was suspicious of holy orders in general and Roman Catholics in particular. None of this, however, made Father Carlo a murderer.

At that moment, his thoughts and the Skype were interrupted by an unknocking Harvey Contractor.

"Sorry to interrupt," he said, not looking at all sorry, "but I've got some info on the padre. I thought you might enjoy it."

"Sorry, Michael," he said. "I'll try to find out about Accrington Stanley, but I fear duty calls." At saying this, he turned off his foreign friend and felt momentarily like God. Less so, however, when Contractor said, "Accrington Stanley, zero; Crewe Alexandra, eight."

"Silly score," he thought, "and two silly names."

"I don't think Father Carlo has ever taken an exam in his life," said Contractor, excited to the extent that he was, in Churchillian argot, intoxicated by his own exuberance.

"What makes you say that?" Bognor was intrigued by the urbane otherworldliness of a certain sort of cleric—usually Roman Catholic, often a Jesuit. He thought of Father Lancelot in Macau with his carefully graded bottles of whiskey and of the suave Mervyn Stockwood who was reputed, as an admittedly Anglican bishop, to have a cellar divided not into clarets and burgundies but wines suitable for laity, clerisy, episcopacy, and royalty. That, at least, was the gossip. He suspected that Father Carlo had just such a cellar and was a little sketchy on the precise theology of, say, transubstantiation. "Better on Saint-Estèphe than Saint John the Divine," he murmured, but Contractor was too bound up in his discoveries to notice.

"You have to pass exams in order to be ordained. Even in the Roman Catholic church," he said.

Bognor had Contractor down as a militant atheist, school of Dawkins, despite his protestations about being open-minded. He himself was characteristically wishy-washy—an Anthony Howard sort of liberal agnostic who enjoyed the noise but was less sure of the content. A message man, not given to massage. Or something like that. He was not sure about Marshall McLuhan but that was almost certainly a red herring. Besides it was the confusion of method and message that defined McLuhan. He was not sure that was Father Carlo's problem.

"No one in this country ever asks questions," Contractor said with enviable certainty. Bognor felt it was much more complicated than that, but this was an important part of a problem Bognor was reluctant to recognize. He always thought life was more complicated than it seemed. Sometimes, however, it was ludicrously simple and the answer was staring him straight in the face. He was one of those people who was reluctant to admit that two and two added up to four. Maybe they did but maybe they didn't. It depended what you meant by two; or indeed by four. This painful ability to see many sides of the most simple puzzle was becoming worse with age. It prevented him rising to the very top of his profession, but paradoxically you could argue that it had also enabled him to get where he was. Life was like that. Complicated.

"The result being that there are a lot of people walking around who have never been asked the simplest things about themselves. The net result is that we have more than our share of conmen. We are not a nation of fact-checkers."

"Vulgar," said Bognor, "like discussing money, especially one's own, and particularly at mealtimes."

Contractor thought vulgarity had something to do, if anything, with fractions.

"If you say so," he said, which was Contractor's way of implying that his boss's ideas went out with the Ark. "But the fact is that we are inclined to let people invent their own curriculum vitae and that isn't always an advantage."

"Honesty is a particularly English virtue. Assuming it in

others is even more so." He knew he sounded pompous or at least sententious. Too bad. It was what he believed. Or had, once upon a time.

"It's led to an epidemic of conmen. If you take things at face value, word gets around. Leads to all sorts of unpleasantness. Most of all taking advantage. All kinds of low life do just that. One doesn't ask questions. Not the done thing, old boy. If someone sports an Eton tie, we assume he is entitled to same. Fact of life."

"I was always brought up to believe that wearing an old school tie was essentially infra dig," Bognor spoke huffily and sounded insufferably pompous. His awareness of this did not make it any easier or any less real. Contractor said nothing. There was no need.

"Acceptance is a peculiarly English vice," he said. "But the church is different. The minute someone sports a dog collar, he is sacrosanct, inviolate. He can get away with murder. Literally."

"Are you implying . . . ?"

"That Father Carlo dunnit?" Contractor affected to think about this as if it were a novelty. "It's possible. Half the popes in history were murderers or rapists. Read John Julius Norwich."

"But Father Carlo . . ."

"Could be our man. I didn't say he *was* our man. That's different."

"You said that Carlo had never passed an exam; that he isn't entitled to fatherhood, as it were."

"Too smooth by half."

Bognor smiled. "Priests who stay with the Jesuits at Farm Street are like that. Particularly ones who are attached to the Frari in Venice. Of course he's smooth. Those two qualifications alone are enough. He has to be smooth. He has to be able to hold his own at dinner in The Connaught; has to be able to snap his fingers at the sommelier; send back the wine when it's corked; know his *rognons* from his sweetbreads, if you follow me. I'll bet he doesn't wear a rough brown habit and open-toed sandals in London."

"If he does, the habit will have been knocked up in Savile Row and the sandals will be from Lobb's not a pair of Mr. Clark's open-toed, mass-produced jobs."

"Precisely," said Bognor. "I can picture him. Typical smart Roman. But that doesn't make him a murderer."

"It does, if allied to ecclesiastical illiteracy. He may be able to do offal in a way that will keep the maître d' at The Connaught happy, but he doesn't know his apostles from his Apocrypha. He thinks Saint John is a little place run by Fergus whatsit."

"Henderson. Top to tail. Most Italian priests of a certain rank are perfectly conversant with fine dining and some of them are a bit shaky when it comes to the sacraments. Father Carlo obviously belongs to that group. You can't make monsignor without cutting the mustard, and your average cardinal is a class act. RC priests in continental Europe aren't like Church of England clergy here." Bognor felt he knew his stuff, and he was only a little out-of-date. That was to do with his time, which was past but only just. In his day, the C of E was the Conservative Party at prayer. Now, like so many Englishmen, he was "lapsed" C of E, but he had been brought up when things were different and when being an Anglican mattered. Nowadays, only the God Squad bothered. Not like Europe where people still went in droves and the parish priest was king even if he had the morals of a monkey.

"I still think Father Carlo is a reprobate even by the standards of the church in Italy," said Contractor, sounding unnaturally pompous especially for one so young. This cheered Bognor profoundly for even when he sounded pompous he was not naturally so.

"Yes. Well, Father Carlo is certainly worth a chat over a glass of good claret, but I think you will find him clean. Not good but clean."

"I still don't think he ever passed an exam."

"That," Bognor said with a certainty that stemmed from the comparative ignorance of his subordinate, "is neither here nor there. It simply isn't about exams. Roman Catholicism isn't like that. Nor Christianity, come to that."

"If God existed," Contractor protested sulkily, "he would expect his representatives on Earth to be properly qualified."

"If Father Carlo really wasn't qualified to represent our Lord in this world, he is making a remarkably good fist of it. Wouldn't you agree?" asked Bognor, who found Father Carlo plausible. Frighteningly so.

"In the sense that he represents God at five-star hotels I

might agree," said Contractor. "I just think he cuts a less impressive figure in the confessional. Not to mention the pulpit."

"I grant you that Father Carlo is a lounge lizard sort of cleric, but we can't all be about hair shirts and flagellation. Even duchesses have faith. Being privileged doesn't bar you from taking part."

"I always subscribe to that stuff about rich men and the eyes of needles," said Contractor, sniffing. "But maybe I'm a purist."

"All we know about the reverend gentleman," said Bognor, "is that he was a friend of the deceased and that he was in the city when he was exterminated. We don't have a vestige of motive, let alone proof."

"Silverburger doesn't strike me as religious. But then nor does Father Carlo."

This was silly. Bognor told him so and backed up his argument with references to Monsignor Ronald Knox, the quintessentially svelte Father Hollins, and Monsignor Gilbey, who had lived at The Travellers Club in Pall Mall and celebrated mass in a broom cupboard there.

"Socially acceptable priests don't go around killing people," Bognor said sententiously. "Rather the reverse. Killing people would be regarded as in very poor taste by those who mattered."

"Quite," agreed Contractor. He was being ironic.

This was not, however, the time nor place for an argument about social mores and the priesthood. There was a murder to solve.

"Did you find anything definite about Father Carlo? Or was it all speculative?"

"We know that he was in Venice on the day of Silverburger's death, during Carnival. We know that he and Silverburger were friends and often ate together. And we know that he enjoyed . . . enjoys . . . dressing up."

"Dressing up," repeated Bognor. "Dressing up, eh?"

"Had his cassocks tailored in Savile Row. Copes from Prada. But no . . ."

"What do you mean, no?" asked Bognor.

"No evidence that he indulged himself at Carnival. No evidence that he ever disguised himself as Harlequin."

"In itself, that proves nothing at all," said Bognor. He was musing, almost thinking out loud, talking to himself.

"Had money," said Contractor. "Well, a bit. For a man of the cloth, he was well off. He was an only child. His father was big in nougat."

"Nougat," Bognor said thoughtfully. "I thought nougat was French. Montélimar." Not many people knew this, but Contractor knew everything that there was to be known.

"This was Italian nougat," he said. "Father Carlo's father was as big as it's possible to get in Italian nougat. The padre was an only child and when his mom and dad were killed in a car crash, he got everything. Not as much as if his old man had been a French nougat baron but not bad. Actually, the Italians think they got there several hundred years before the French. Real nougat originally came from Cremona. The French stole the idea of mixing egg whites and honey from the Italians and passed it off as their own. Typical. In Italy, it's called *mandolato*, which isn't as catchy. But the taste is the same. Anyway, Father Carlo came into a considerable amount of dosh. For a priest, it was a very tidy sum indeed. Enough to buy dinner, flash it around some pretty spectacular high-rolling joints, and enough to back Silverburger, if not exactly bankroll him."

"And did he?"

"What? Back him? Yes, in a quiet, unflashy sort of way. He put up the money for an initial purchase or two. Paid for a treatment. That sort of thing."

"I see," said Bognor. He didn't, of course, but took refuge in the phrase that made him feign omniscience. He didn't fool many people and certainly not Contractor. Contractor may have got a phony-sounding qualification from a new-fangled university, but this didn't prevent him from being quite bright.

"Silverburger had been taking church money for a variety of projects for at least a decade."

"That still doesn't make Father Carlo a murderer," said Bognor.

"No," agreed his minion. "But it means he was involved with Silverburger. In fact, he was up to his neck. Not just a passing acquaintance or even a dining companion. He was a business associate, and we all know what that can mean."

"Business sounds shady before we begin," said Bognor, "and I admit that I have an aversion to business in every shape and form. On the other hand, I'm man enough to admit my prejudice. I know enough about banking to understand that not all bankers are villains. Jolly nearly all bankers. And I do think there is something inherently wrong about moneylending, making vast amounts of the stuff and indeed in talking about it. But on the other hand, spondulicks makes the world go round. Sort of. Up to a point. On the other hand, possession of too much of the stuff is nine-tenths of the way to . . ."

"Careful," said Contractor, smiling. "You're in danger of showing your prejudices."

"Oh, all right," agreed his boss. "But I do prefer my friars to be . . . well, Franciscan."

13

"I think you're indulging yourself," said Monica, smothering beef in béarnaise. "Brunetti and Zen likewise. Venice is a tourist destination. Historic, beautiful but safe as houses. Nice place to visit, but nothing happens there."

"You're exaggerating," said Bognor. She did this habitually. She thought it helped. Bognor found it endearing; Monica's enemies, of whom there were many, found the habit exasperating.

"Those bandits from Africa selling handbags that fell off the backs of trucks; they're the nearest to serious crime that Venice gets. Tourists are natural victims, and Venice-recidivists tend to have more money than sense. I suppose a certain sort of tart and her pimp move in for the Biennale, but that's about it. The only reason people such as Donna Leon write about the place is that they enjoy being there. Don't blame them. You enjoy it; Michael is one your oldest friends; you enjoy *carpaccio* and the Danieli, but nothing ever happens there. It's part of its charm—all past and no future. Not even much of a present. On the other hand, the smell, the decay, the accumulation of doges and expats, make it irresistible. Byron has a lot to answer for."

"That's not fair." He was eating steak, too. The table-cloth was check, and there was a wax candle on the table. The place reminded both Bognors of the Paris of their youth. The prices had increased exponentially, but everything else was much the same. Age had made them gastronomically conservative, though not politically so. In this, they were odd.

"Crime crops up in the least expected places. It is a complete fallacy to think that murder is peculiar to the drab and deprived."

She snorted. "I know that. It's just that Venice is a safe house. And you like it. So do I. And one of the reasons I enjoy going there is that I don't feel threatened. I don't deny that Silverburger was murdered, but his death doesn't represent the beginning of a crime wave. He deserved it. He was a nasty piece of work, and his demise docsn't deserve your interest. He wasn't worth it. You know that, and the only reason that you're making such a meal of it, is that it suits you. His murder gives you an excuse to do what you enjoy most—

having nice meals in beautiful places with friends. I'm not denying the attraction, just asking you not to pretend. This isn't work. It's pleasure."

Bognor wiped the last of the béarnaise and the gravy (which was still gravy but was now called *jus*) with a slice of bread and gave the impression of thought.

"You aren't being fair. Silverburger may not have been nice; he may even have been a nasty piece of work, but he was still a human being and, were it not for me, his death would go relatively unmourned and uninvestigated."

"That," she said, slurping Beaujolais, "is unfair to Michael."

"Ah," said Bognor, "one minute you accuse me of being fond of Michael, the next you attack me for being unfair to him. He was the one who asked me for assistance."

"I can have it both ways," she said. "That's a woman's pre-rogative. Besides which, you told me that Michael asked for help, but I only have your word for it. I'm not convinced that it's in his nature to seek assistance. He's too proud. Typical Italian."

"Michael is many things but typical isn't one of them. He's a perfectly good copper and he'll ask for help when it's relevant and necessary. As it is in the murder of Irving Silverburger."

"You're being silly," she said, but despite this, she loved him. Really. "Coffee?" she asked, almost solicitously. They both had a double espresso as well as one for the road. There were too many roads in their lives.

Over calvados and coffee, they discussed Venice, murder,

the meaning of life, and whether or not the exercise had been worthwhile. Theirs was a typical conversation of those at their time of life.

"I still think Venice is safe," said Monica, "and Doyle was wrong. There is nothing sinister about the countryside. Most crimes take place in slums and deprived areas. Most of those who write about killing are middle class, and they know nothing about such things. Hence their obsession with the countryside, with the upper classes and places like Venice. Hence *Midsomer Murders*. Hence Aurelio Zen."

"Venice isn't like anywhere else. And there is nothing 'typical' about the typical English village. English villages don't do typical any more than Michael."

"Touché," said Monica. "But you must agree that most crime is dull. The average thief belongs to a small company with a van and a couple of crowbars. Killing people in unpleasant surroundings is commonplace. I think P. D. James was right. Murder is working class. It's the rarity in middle- and upper-class England, which helps make it interesting. And Venice. In real life, they don't occur where they do in fiction. Fact of death."

She drank coffee and looked smug. They had been married a long time and always to each other. That, too, was unusual.

"So you think killing people is not just wrong but squalid. Necessarily so."

She thought for a moment. "Yes," she said. "Yes, I suppose I do."

"So you feel I've spent most of my working life grappling with the squalid."

She did some more thinking and sipping and said, "If you put it like that, then yes, I suppose I do. But that's not at all the same as saying you've wasted your time. On the contrary, someone has to resolve life's unpleasantness and it's a noble cause. So just because I think you've spent most of your life fighting squalor isn't at all the same as saying that no one should do so. Fighting crime is good. We need more graduates doing it. One of the problems of the police is that they have no graduate-entry scheme; no proper officer class; and they set store by pounding beat rather than exercising little gray cells. In real life, the odds are against intelligence."

"Hmmm," said Bognor. "So crime in Venice is a form of tautology."

"Which isn't the same as saying it doesn't happen; nor that it isn't entertaining and surprising when it does."

"So my investigations in Venice are superfluous?"

"Let's just say," she said, "that there is more crime north of the Trent than to the south; that working-class Glasgow has more violence than Belgravia. Irving Silverburger is an intriguing death and a better class of corpse than you get in the Gorbals. That's not at all the same as saying that he is not a cause for lamentation or that we shouldn't solve his murder. If murder it is. Not a lot of pavement cafés north of the Watford Gap. Don't pretend you would rather be in Venice than, say, Bradford."

"I've never been to Bradford."

"Don't be silly. You know what I mean."

He did, too.

"It's not self-indulgent to try to solve Silverburger's murder. You could say the reverse. Not many people have the opportunity."

"Now you really are being silly. Don't tell me you'd rather be thinking about crossbowed film directors over a Negroni than considering a drug death over a pint of mild and bitter."

"They don't drink mild and bitter up north anymore. Besides I never touch alcohol on duty."

"Liar," she said affectionately. "You practically invented the three-martini lunch."

"That was in the sixties," he protested. "Times have changed."

"Not for you they haven't," said his wife. "You think they're still happening. You believe pop music is the Beatles. It's like having dinner here. Most people find change difficult. You enjoy the comforts of the familiar. You want everything to stay the same even if you disapprove of it. Like crime. You want fingerprints and deference, helmets, boys in blue, and other ranks calling you 'sir.'"

"Probably," he agreed. "When we were young, I was passionately opposed to the ancient because they seemed to expect a respect that they hadn't earned. They expected us to scrape and bow simply because we were young and they were old. Nowadays, being old is a bad joke; you're on the shelf at forty, and people don't even stand up for you in crowded tube trains."

"Someone stood for me on the Northern Line from Kings Cross the other day," said Monica. "I was livid. And he was in school uniform. Could have killed him. Almost did."

"Why does no train manager ever ask me for my senior citizen's railcard?" complained Bognor. "After all, I don't look like a senior citizen, do I?"

"No, darling," agreed Lady Bognor. "Even quite young people are blotchy, thin on top and gray at the temples."

"Bitch," Bognor said affectionately. "At least women are allowed to dye their hair."

"And wear wigs," said Monica.

Her husband stared at her. "You, never," he said. "A wig. That's shocking. I'm shocked."

"Cherie Blair wears a wig," said Monica, "and she's younger than me. Much."

"That's the sort of thing you pick up on Twitter," said the head of SIDBOT, who did not believe in social networking but liked to do his face to face, man to man, over a stiff something or other. "You're the sort of person who believes what people say on Twitter."

"I do not." This was really insulting, much the worst thing Simon had said that evening. All week indeed. "I heard it at the hairdresser's."

Even Monica had to have her hair cut. In the salon, she listened to gossip, some of which she believed. Bognor mocked this; he would; he was a man.

"Same thing as Twitter. In any case, just because I like Venice and enjoy Michael's company doesn't mean it's not work."

"Of course not."

"You said I was only working on the case because I enjoyed the place and Michael. Both happen to be true but that's not why I'm involved on the case. Silverburger was murdered. It's up to me to establish who did it."

"Yes, darling." She smiled a superior smile. It spoke volumes. Not very good ones. In fact, more than a trace of bodice ripper or at least Mills and Boon, but lots of books.

"Why don't you say, 'Well, someone has to do it?' " she continued. "You usually do. And no one else is going to."

He called for the bill, which he would pay, even though they shared an account so that this was a facade and really just window dressing. There were some things, however, a man had to do. Even if deference was a thing of the past and train managers were younger than bishops, didn't mean one had to give up.

"If I didn't solve upper- and middle-class crime, then the upper and middle classes would get away with murder."

"That's effectively the same thing. Just expressed differently."

"What?" He had forgotten. The Beaujolais and calvados had gone to his head. "The point is there's a murderer at large."

"Yes, darling."

"And he could strike again at any moment."

"That I doubt," she said. "That's part of what I mean. Silverburger's killing was an aberration, a one-off. It won't happen again. Some maniac is not going to take out his crossbow and go on a rampage up and down La Serenissima. Silver-burger's killer won't strike again. He only wanted to kill one person. He's not a serial killer. Not someone from Sheffield or the Gorbals. Not a real pro."

"Doesn't mean I don't have to bring him to justice," he said.

"Ah." She looked dangerously thoughtful. "It depends what you mean by justice. Our murderer might have justice on his side. Only he took it into his own hands. So perhaps he was right. Maybe he had to kill Silverburger and bringing him to justice not only serves no purpose but is wrong in its own right, if you follow my drift."

The bill came. It was huge, but Bognor paid little attention. After all, it was only money and half was hers, half the eating and drinking as well. Theirs was a shared experience, jointly paid for. There was no room for recrimination.

Even so, Simon felt his wife's strictures were unfair. He had, after all, always mixed business with pleasure; always fought unpopular corners and enjoyed doing so. He had done a good job, had fun while doing so, made some friends and even more enemies. This was a sound definition of a life well led, and he was tolerably well satisfied. Not self-satisfied, which implied smug, which he deplored.

If he wished to investigate the criminal death of a widely disliked quasi-American would-be film mogul, so be it. He felt entitled. And he was not having anyone, even Monica, gainsaying him.

"I wouldn't normally say this," he said as they stood, "but let's take a cab for once."

She smiled. He always said this and had done for more than thirty years.

Bognor seemed to conduct an unacceptable proportion of his investigative interviews over meals. And he drank on duty, though never at breakfast. Partly because he wanted to educate Contractor, partly because he felt challenged, he offered his subordinate breakfast at The Connaught just as his organization had offered the priest the same meal in the same place. This time, Bognor paid. Personally.

Alcohol loosened the tongue. It also induced confidence and a lowering of the guard. Kidneys or kedgeree were palatable substitutes but not, in his experience, as good as a glass of Grange. He paused from self-examination to reflect that his interviewing technique was only "unacceptable" in the early years of the twenty-first century. It had been thought perfectly normal when he was growing up, and it was only now that it had become freakish and not quite the done thing. It was the same with people such as young Contractor accusing him of having an alcohol problem. He had no such problem, and it was only latterly that regular consumption of the stuff had become problematic. Time was when everyone drank. They died younger but were therefore less of a burden on the state and their families. Good show. Like smoking.

Bognor sighed and speared a sausage. In some ways, he hankered for the "good old days." He knew perfectly well that they were old and not necessarily good, but that was too bad. In many ways, he preferred them. Everyone cared less for the peripheral, and they were not as selfish as they had become. Privately, he and his wife thought the modern generation a dull lot.

Not that this was an accusation that could be leveled at Father Carlo. He was a priest of the old school, which is to say that he was not a priest in any serious sense. Religion was not something that sat heavily on his shoulders, if indeed it could be said to sit at all. Harvey Contractor speared a sausage in much the same way as Bognor. The reverend gentleman ate sausages in a similar fashion.

"One of the aspects of British life that I most value is the sausage," said Contractor. Like Father Carlo, he came from somewhere else, but he was a fanatical Anglophile and he correctly prided himself on his command of colloquial English. "Or banger. I have never understood why 'banger.' My sausages seldom bang. Indeed, you could say with conviction that they never bang."

"Like the crossbow," said Bognor. "No bang. No telltale puff of smoke. No whiff of cordite. Our chaps showed foreigners what was what with their long bows at the Battle of Agincourt. But they were specialist archers. A man with a crossbow does not require special skills. Anyone can handle a crossbow, and it leaves no trace. Lethal and all things to all men."

"I agree," said Contractor, munching, "and I could perfectly well have killed Silverburger if I were in Venice the day he was shot. And if I may say so, the disguise is perfect. The weapon is silent, its carriage would have excited no comment, its use and accuracy would have been no hurdle for an enthusiastic amateur. Well, even for an apathetic amateur, since you ask. So yes, I had the methodology. Unfortunately, I was at work in London. Motive, however, is another matter even for the padre. Why would he have wished him dead?" He went on munching but looked thoughtful.

"There is a widespread feeling that Silverburger was not terribly nice."

"Carlo thought he was perfectly nice. But then he would. They have a maxim in the Church about not speaking ill of the dead. But he was a friend. Any friend is, in my opinion, nice. That is what friendship is about. It's about thinking people nice even if the world thinks otherwise."

Bognor nodded. He was unable to speak, partly because his mouth was full of sausage and partly because he was over-whelmed by Contractor's effrontery and suaveness. He was asking him to believe that the Roman Catholics had some sort of monopoly on the dead and also, by implication, that he knew more about friendship than he, Bognor. Bognor was rather strong on such notions as loyalty, friendship, and the fickleness of fashion. He stuck to his friends no matter what. Actually, a bit of no matter what, worked wonders. Bognor was never so fiercely loyal as when the world turned sour.

"Quite," he said when he had swallowed the morsel of sausage and composed himself. Contractor was dreadfully plausible, even if one would not want, in Field Marshal Montgomery's well-observed maxim, to go into the jungle with him.

"So the motive is difficult."

"I couldn't have put it better myself," said Contractor, though Bognor wasn't aware of any particularly felicitous phraseology. "Many, many people had the opportunity, but motive is something else. You would know this more than I, myself. But I am acquainted with motive. Most men of God are in that difficult position, especially in the Catholic Church. It is the product of the confessional."

Bognor supposed that your average RC chap heard more individual sin in that curious box than the average C of E minister, let alone any other denominations. He simply didn't know about Muslims and others. Did Muslims confess? And if so, to whom? Discuss.

"In my experience, knowing someone at all well is the beginnings of motive. Or to put it another way, it is not usual for complete strangers to kill one another."

Contractor seemed surprised. "I hadn't thought of it quite like that," he said. "They say a little knowledge is a dangerous thing, but I am not certain that this is what is meant. No knowledge at all does seem to rule out murder. Thank heaven, you are able to narrow the field. Without that, you would have suspicions of everyone who attended Carnival that day. Whereas . . ."

"Whereas?" repeated Bognor.

"On the other hand, knowledge is not enough in itself. One must have a reason, mustn't one? Unless this was a random killing. I have heard of random killings, but I have never encountered one. If this was a random killing, you have a different problem, and there is also an increased chance that the murderer might kill a second time. Would you not agree? If the killing was motivated by a reason that had nothing to do with the identity of the one killed, then there is an increased likelihood that he may, as they say, strike again."

"He or she," he said.

It was his subordinate's turn to say "quite." He did so.

"It is a widely held belief that priests who have no carnal relations are hermaphrodites. Even if this were the case, he would be able to handle a crossbow. This was one of the essential differences between the English and the European weapon. The English archer was a specialist; the European could have been anyone because the crossbow was a lowest common denominator. Anyone could handle it. It took a strong man with finely honed arms. Muscles were indispensable. Technique likewise."

Bognor could not fail to be impressed. The present pope had closed down a Cistercian community after the monks had been found operating lap dancers, a twenty-four hour service, and embezzling funds. They were probably involved in arranging the venues for the World Cup Soccer Finals. Rotten old pope. What a killjoy!

"To be a servant of the Lord does not mean one is immune from the devil's temptations," said Contractor, spearing a recalcitrant kidney.

"Quite," agreed Bognor. "However, being a servant of the Lord does mean that one doesn't succumb. Being a servant of the Lord confers no immunity, but it does confer obligations."

Bognor was rather pleased with this especially when Contractor regarded him with what seemed awfully like respect. This could have had something to do with the fact that Bognor was picking up the tab. He topped up both coffees.

"As a general rule," said Bognor, "Roman Catholic priests are regarded as more worldly. Despite the fact that they are technically celibate."

"Technically."

"So you don't believe priests are always celibate?"

"I was merely echoing what you said. You could put it down to politeness."

"I won't, though," said Bognor. "Even priests are only polite when it suits them."

"This is very intriguing but not the point," said his guest, "which is that Father Carlo had ample opportunity but no discernible motive."

"The confessional conceals much," said Bognor. "Even motive. And the secrecy that attaches to it is often inimical to the truth. I'm afraid we don't deal with the spiritual. Nor in that sense does the Church of England. In our church, everything is open and above board. We have no secrets from one another. We are on the same side. The Roman church is different. At times, one could say that it plays on the opposing team."

"We, too, believe in justice. However, ours is a more eternal notion; here is gone tomorrow, now is illusory. The Lord's right and the Lord's wrong are forever. Above all, it isn't usurped by mere mortals. God's law is superior to man's. Even your church believes that."

"Our church may preach that, but in practice it is what we describe as law abiding. For Anglicans, the law is the law and right is right."

"There is a danger of your people equating right with might," said the younger man. "We, on the other hand, are meek and powerless. The pope has no battalions. God's army carries no weapons."

"I won't beat about the bush," said Bognor. "I believe that he could have had a motive. On the other hand, your church won't allow you to incriminate yourself if, in doing so, you break the vow of the confessional."

"Oh, come, come." Contractor spread butter and marmalade on his toast. A lot of it. More than was good for him. More than God would like.

"If he had a motive," said Bognor, "he would not tell me. The same as doctors. They have a let-out. Faith is stronger than patriotism."

"I'm sorry?"

"We don't agree; we don't believe but there is nothing we can do about it."

"We believe in justice in a temporal as well as an eternal sense. This is important. The church is not obstructive. It is a force for good." He bit into the toast.

"Ever since they were in the seminary as boys, they must have been friends . . . like brothers . . ."

At this, for the first time, Bognor crunched into an approximation of alertness.

"Seminary?" he said. "Silverburger?"

"You knew." Contractor seemed genuinely shocked. "In Missouri. Isolated community outside Saint Louis. Poor Irving lost his vocation, though I'm not sure he was ever properly chosen. It was force of circumstance. Irving was more of an orphan than an acolyte, if you follow me. He was always a little wayward. Lapsed. Very."

So Silverburger was lapsed, a Catholic who had lost his calling and a lifelong friend of Father Carlo since they were students in the same seminary way back. Bognor remembered saying that total strangers rarely killed each other and never with a crossbow during a Venetian Carnival. Father Carlo might have shriven the deceased, given him a few Ave Marias to recite, or whatever confessors did. He would have remained, probably, a relative stranger and bound by the oaths of the confessional. However, he was a friend and not only a friend but one of long standing. And friends, even old ones, were bound by nothing at all. What's more, friendship may not have made Father Carlo a killer, but it increased his rating as a suspect. Interesting. Very interesting. Bognor looked at the bill, frowned briefly, but considered it, on the whole, money well spent.

14

The priest was oleaginous, but that did not make him a murderer. He had known Irving Silverburger when they were both seminarians. Silverburger had lost his vocation even if he had not previously found it. Father Carlo . . . Father Carlo's vocation was doubtful, even if professed and turned to advantage. That did not mean that he had shot his old friend with a crossbow. The facts were beginning to stack up, though they only fed Bognor's prejudices.

Thus he mused on a crowded London pavement that morning after breakfast. He had paid; therefore he walked. Contractor had other fish. Bognor was not a great believer in exercise and, on the whole, subscribed to the school of thought that had a large drink and a good lie-in whenever the notion of beneficial physical exertion was suggested. That way, the urge would soon pass. It had to be said though that it was an urge Bognor seldom experienced. And for a man of his age, he was in pretty good shape. He had a certain short-ness of breath when running—as good a reason as any for avoiding exercise of all kinds. There was a certain tendency to portliness and a slight heightening of a naturally pink ten-dency. Bognor put all this down to a natural concomitant of advancing years and liked to think that it enhanced the pos-sibility of respect. This seemed to him in short supply, but he was man enough to put a lack of deference down to reasons other than age and lack of fitness.

Mrs. Thatcher had uttered some spurious adage about public transport and lack of success but, quite apart from the fact that he had an illogical aversion to everything about Mrs. Thatcher, he didn't think she had said anything about walk-ing. In fact, Bognor took public transport whenever possible on the grounds that he liked to feel close to his fellow human beings, besides which he enjoyed cocking a snook at Thatch-erite thought, even if Thatcherite thinkers persisted in not noticing. Besides, he liked ambling along crowded London pavements.

Odd how prejudiced one could be. Forensically, he knew that Father Carlo was no more or less likely to have killed his old friend and yet, because he disliked him, he suspected that he was a murderer. Rationally, Bognor knew that this was wrong and that his suspicions were entirely visceral. And yet,

they persisted. He disliked mumbo jumbo, he hated hypocrisy, and he felt Father Carlo embodied both. He was, however, sufficiently professional to recognize prejudice for what
it was. On the other hand, he had a lot of respect for gut
feeling, and he believed that it was something to do with this
that raised common or garden detectives to greatness. Actually, this was an across-the-board sort of belief. He had a lot of
faith in the common man, but what made the common man
uncommon was a factor that was inimical to analysis and had
a lot to do with character and gut or possibly what the writer
Joseph Conrad had described as "Ability in the abstract." He
would like to see that debated. Years ago, he probably would
have seen it debated. His belief was that methodology and
hard work counted for a great deal in this life but was beta
stuff unless touched by genius. Or something.

Thus he mused as he slouched along toward his Bethle-
hem of an office. The crowds were thick and alien. London,
since he had first lived there, had become infinitely more cosmopolitan, and although he felt far from the British National
Party, duskier and more alien. There was more than a hint of
yashmaks in the air, men with whiskers smoked hookahs at
outside cafés, and people spoke no known language. Bognor
felt ill at ease. He was so very English. Everyone else was so
very not.

The part prejudice played in detection was remarkable.
He knew that the book was good and that rules were inevitable, but the really good cop knew when to throw away the
book and to abandon the rules. He thought of himself as a

really good cop and despite believing in rules and books, he felt he knew when to abide by them and when to trust his waters, his instinct, call it what you will. Right now, however, he was unsure. He knew he disliked the priest and he also disliked the shifting sands on which he stood. He was, however, man enough to concede that this was prejudice. Sometimes he trusted this; at other times not. Right now, however, he simply did not know and uncertainty was no sort of forensic passport. The great detective was always incisive. He did not dither.

Bognor sidestepped a twin baby carriage pushed by a girl in a yashmak who looked at him balefully with kohl-rimmed eyes while her two children chattered to each other amiably in a language with which he was unfamiliar. London had become exotic. Men like Silverburger and Father Carlo felt more at home there than Bognor. Even the shop signs were often in characters he did not understand. His city had been hijacked. He did not like it.

The fact remained that the death of Irving G. Silverburger was not at the top of anyone's agenda. It was probably not at the top of Bognor's own agenda nor even that of Michael Dibdini. The film mogul's death could safely be shunted away, stuffed under the carpet of life, and left there. Nobody cared for him in life, and nobody cared for him in death. Sometimes, Bognor felt it was his role to stand up for the boy who would otherwise be consigned to the corner of the classroom and left there while his colleagues went out to play.

Benito, the gondolier, he thought to himself. Why not a gondolier? Men such as Bognor believed that men such as Benito, the gondolier, were clichés in Venice. They thought that gondoliers were inevitably working class, though this probably did not matter as much as their foreignness, their lack of Englishness. Bognor was not class conscious, but he was inclined to xenophobia. Benito was common in much the same way as your average taxi driver, but Bognor had nothing against the old-fashioned driver of a black cab who had done that curious exam known as "the knowledge" and which seemed to involve scootering around a deserted city on a Sunday with a clipboard attached to the handlebars. Salt of the earth, that sort of taxi driver. Knew his way around London, knew what was what, knew his place in society. Not like the spivs who drove minicabs, unregistered, subject to no exams or regulations of any kind. They did not know their way around London and often spoke little or no English. They were foreign.

He, however . . . No, he must not do that. He had to blend and not be noticed. It was bad form in any number of ways to stand out in a crowd and also distinctly unprofessional. One of the more important characteristics of detective work was the ability to enter any world and not to attract attention or elicit gossip. Anonymity was all.

So he ambled back to his desk where he summoned Contractor who yearned to be his master's everything but was at least his legs. He did most of the running around. Bognor was increasingly sedentary. Contractor must have taken the bus. Thatcher would not have approved.

"You called, Boss," said Contractor, smiling sycophanti-
cally. Bognor liked to think that he remained the essential
brains in this operation and that made him indispensable.
Yet he was also sufficiently self-aware to realize that he was
approaching his sell-by date even if he was not actually quite
there yet. The place of the elder statesman in any society was
always more appreciated by the old and, arguably, wise. But
it was more and more at risk. Progressives put this down to a
general belt-tightening, but Bognor and his generation were
not so sure. The presence of the old and bold lent texture and
gravitas to any organization. Even if it was not particularly
desirable that important decisions should be left to the weary
and indecisive, there was a limit to the efficacy of the young
and thrusting. Youth was all very well in its way, but it had a
certain headless quality. Contractor was excellent at energy
but less so at wisdom. Short on deference as well, but that
was something else.

"What do you know about gondoliers?" asked Bognor.

"Always been very suspicious," said Contractor. "They
strike me as being parasites preying on the body of La Serenissima. They feed a demand, but it isn't a healthy demand
and nor are they. That's my view anyway. I am sure there are
some perfectly nice gondoliers, but I just don't know any. But
then, I don't know any nice taxi drivers. Or bankers."

"Are you equating gondoliers with bankers and taxi drivers?"

Contractor thought about this, or gave every indication of
doing so. Eventually, he said, "In the sense that they're spivs
and that they exploit honest hardworking citizens, I suppose

I am. So, yes. I'm sure there are exceptions, but they only go to prove the rule. I daresay there is such a thing as an acceptable gondolier, but most gondoliers are not. They are part of the unacceptable face of tourism. Part of the unacceptable face of Venice."

SIDBOT did not like priests or gondoliers. They stood for something in society—these two people—for they were visible and in their own showy way, they mattered. In Bognor's overall scheme of things, they could not have mattered less; nor in Harvey Contractor's, which was part of the reason for Bognor liking the younger man and for feeling that when he was gone, the outfit was in safe hands. They both disliked the ostentatious; in their very different ways, the priest and the gondolier were more about show than substance. They pretended to be the servant of everyman while, not so secretly, believing themselves to be superior. The one doffed and tugged, bowed and scraped, and rowed rich tourists about his city; the other heard man's misdeeds on behalf of his employer in the ancient anonymity of his wooden box, set the newly shriven a Hail Mary or two in the name of the Lord and smirked to heaven. Both appeared to be menials but actually believed themselves to be superior beings.

Bognor had known prefects such as that at school. Teachers, too. Even the headmaster had preached servitude while practicing superiority. If authority were questioned, authority reacted in a predictable reactionary way. If you suggested that the man in charge of the vessel was using his pole in the wrong way, or that the priest was lacking in his knowledge of the scriptures, the men would call "time out" and protest that the heckling itself was a breach of some unformulated rule known only to them. This was humbug. It was recognized as such by Bognor and his subordinate. They both disliked it and the fact that it ruled the world.

Even so it did not make the practitioners into killers. Hypocrites, yes. And the worst sort, too. Arrogant men pretending to be humble; the Uriah Heaps of life. Yet no one dared to point out that they were wearing the emperor's new clothes. The smug inherited the earth and especially those who pretended to be subjects but were actually monarchs. Nevertheless, that did not make such men murderers.

"Didn't like Father Carlo. Greedy. Eyes like a pig. Sweaty hands." Thus Bognor. "Didn't care for the way he ate breakfast. No holding back. Men of the cloth should practice fastidiousness. They should at least seem to be humble. Arrogance is never attractive, especially in servants of the Lord."

"Nor in servants of mammon," said Contractor. "At least bankers are upfront about it. Gondoliers pretend to be interested in their craft while actually only caring for the color of their passengers' money."

"I suppose gondoliers are like waiters," mused Bognor. "They wring their hands, bend double, walk backward, and yet we are all terrified of them. It's a farce, a charade."

"Wine waiters more than the food guys," Contractor said with feeling. A sommelier had once refused to serve him an Argentinian chardonnay on the grounds that it was ghastly. When Contractor had protested that it was cheap and on the list, the sommelier had shrugged as if to suggest that he knew best—better than those who compiled the list and certainly better than the common customer, especially one whose girlfriend was too nubile and obviously unearned. Contractor, who had been intent on impressing the blonde, was humiliated but too ignorant to answer back.

"Don't like them," he said, echoing his master's thoughts, "but that doesn't make them murderers."

15

Bognor rang Venice. Dibdini answered.

"Benito, the gondolier," said Bognor.

"*Sì*," said Dibdini, "the gondolier, Benito."

"You have interviewed him?"

"Of course. He had sex with Silverburger. He is a suspect."

"Because he had sex with the deceased?"

Bognor could almost feel his old friend spreading his hands in a gesture of exasperation. Bognor didn't do exasperation to anyone except his wife, and he didn't spread his hands even for her. Foreign sentiment; extremely foreign gesture.

"I didn't mean that," he said, trying to appear emollient. "Just wondered what you thought."

"I didn't like him."

That meant depressingly little. Both men had a soft spot for murderers. Given a choice between a killer and a thief or swindler, much less a law-abiding member of the public, he and Michael would rather the killer any day. Killers had chutzpah. Those who didn't would like to but hadn't the guts. Detectives had more in common with those they chased than those they were supposed to protect.

"Weasel," said Dibdini. "He was a rodent. Predatory. I don't think he would kill; he was more of a scavenger. I do not believe he would have any moral scruples about killing, but I do believe he would lack the essential bravery. He seemed too cowardly. I do not believe he murdered our friend."

"Silverburger was not our friend. I am operating on a matter of principle."

The Italian did not deal in such abstracts; did not believe in morality, in right or wrong except when confronted by such attributes in human form. He knew a villain when he saw one, but he did not recognize villainy. This did not make him a bad policeman. On the contrary. He was, however, not as good in debate as his English counterpart and certainly could not hold a candle to Contractor. Dibdini thought of semiotics as some sort of pasta. Bognor liked his food, but he was motivated by morality when it came to his work. He was an expert at good and evil, though he was unconvinced by the idea that there was such a thing as a bad man. There were, indubitably, bad things, but Bognor believed they were not done by inherently bad people. In this, he differed from his Italian friend.

"Berlusconi's a bad bugger," Michael would mutter when he had drunk too much grappa. Bognor shared the disapproval but believed that the Italian politician was simply misguided. He was not necessarily a bad man; just one who had mislaid his moral compass.

For Dibdini, Benito the gondolier was a bad man. End of story. Bognor, on the other hand, thought the boatman had taken a wrong turn. From time to time, Dibdini remonstrated, suggesting that a character was beyond redemption. Bognor believed implicitly that the sin was reprehensible and should be punished. On the other hand, he did not subscribe to the idea of the sinner. The Venetian policeman considered the two as indistinguishable. Bad men did bad things, and society should be protected from them. Bognor believed that there was good in everyone and that even the person who had committed the foulest crimes was capable of being reformed. Dibdini thought this fanciful nonsense and that it cluttered the mind.

"So Benito is in London?"

"He is in Colindale. His uncle operates a taxi company. Benito is driving for his uncle, or so he claims. That, as you would say, is his story. However, his uncle pays very little money. The family has a reputation for being less than generous. It is my belief that Benito makes money from sex. He is a male prostitute. He goes with such as the late

Silverburger. He is, as you would say, a for-hire person. His body is the only thing that he is able to offer. So he hires himself for sex."

"A rent boy."

"If you say so."

Bognor did. He knew, too, that Dibdini was quite familiar with the phrase. Venice might be relatively free of murder and mayhem but it was full of rent boys and girls. Sex was universal and it often came at a price.

"So Benito is driving a taxi?"

This sudden turn of direction clearly took his old friend by surprise.

"Benito," he said, "is driving a car. Like Benito's body, it is available. At a price. You pay the money, and Benito is yours for an hour or what you pay. Same with the car."

For some reason, Bognor was reminded of the backwoods Tory member of Parliament of Neanderthal disposition who was told that there was a new brothel within easy reach of Westminster. In this place, you could have a woman and a bottle of claret for a mere thirty pounds or something suitably modest. The knight of the shire wrinkled his nose and said, "Must be bloody awful wine!"

Now Bognor found himself saying, "Benito may be able to drive, but he does not know his way around London. He hasn't even done 'the knowledge.'"

This made him seem as reactionary in his attitude as the notional Tory member of Parliament, which he was not. Actually, Bognor liked to think of himself as to the left of center. This was not a view widely shared, particularly by those younger than himself.

"Benito drives a taxicab because this gives him what you might call respectability. It is similar to being a gondolier here in Venice. It is what you would call 'a cover' for his other activities. Sex is a great deal more lucrative than driving a machine, even a gondola. Sex is worth money, and it can be fun. Perhaps we should all have been prostitutes."

Bognor was shocked by this and said so. Actually, he said, "Taxi driving in London is shocking. Half the drivers speak no English and know Khartoum or Cartagena better than London. Say what you like about old-fashioned black-cab drivers, but they knew their job."

He felt Dibdini acquiesce. "However," pointed out the Italian, "the old-fashioned taxi man did not offer sex."

"Quite right," said Bognor, who was still feeling outraged. "One job at a time is quite enough, and it helps to be able to do that job well. I'm far from convinced that Benito is good at either."

As he uttered this judgment, he realized that he seemed to be condoning prostitution; could at least be thought to be doing so.

"Not," he added hastily, "that I think one should muddle up driving with sex."

"Benito is better at the one than the other," said the Italian, "which is to say that he understands his own body better than he understands the automobile, which is some- one else's."

"Helps to know where you're going," Bognor remarked drily. "When it comes to sex, the result is always the same. The conclusion is therefore satisfactory. When it comes to driving about London, it's a crapshoot. You could get anywhere at all, by any means available. Exciting. Unpredictable. Unlike bed with Benito. I should imagine sexual congress with Benito is a sad business whereas driving in the back of his car carries a certain risk and excitement. I know which I'd rather do."

"You English are all the same," said Michael. "You would prefer to drive in the back of a car than experience the amorous adventures of the boudoir."

"That's ridiculous," said Bognor, who had a robust no-nonsense attitude to sex, typical of his class, generation, gender, and nationality. He and Monica engaged in coital activity in the missionary position, once or twice a week with the lights off. Anything more adventurous was foreign and mildly disgusting. Like aftershave or washing more than necessary.

Benito had a foreigner's enthusiasm for bodily functions. Likewise Silverburger. One bought; the other sold. The transaction was, to Bognor's eye, extremely un-English and, like so many things, probably constituted a beatable offense. Ultimately, though, it was sad. Bognor was not by nature judgmental; nor was he uncharitable. He did not believe in throwing stones, knowing only too well that he was likely to come off second best in any stone-throwing competition. Nor was he sexually greedy. It seemed to him that one person was more than enough for the most self-indulgent libido and also that some sort of monogamy was socially desirable all around. He found it sad when such was not the case; particularly when what should, in his view, have an element of spirituality or at least friendship, and a certain mutual incredulity or at least amusement should become a matter of commercial transaction. He took the view that sex was absolutely not to do with money.

This was obviously not the view of Silverburger or of Benito, the gondolier. It was sadder by the fact that the one had so little to sell and the other so little to offer, except for cash. It was, he supposed, ever thus. It was not in his nature to be censorious about this, but it still made him a little sad. The thought of Benito in bed made him shudder slightly; Silverburger likewise. But then the reality of sexual congress invariably had a quality of absurdity about it. He never gave a second thought to what Monica and he got up to in bed, but he had to concede that outsiders would find their coupling disgusting or risible, possibly both and only mildly so, but only an imbecile or an extreme optimist would think otherwise. Sex was not a dignified occupation even if it was, for most people, commonplace and usual. Best not to think about it.

On the other hand, Benito the gondolier sold it and Silverburger bought it. That may have been sad, but it did not mean that the former was a murderer or, come to that, that his being a commercial consumer constituted an invitation for Silverburger to be shot with a crossbow bolt on his way to the airport in the middle of Carnival.

Bognor frowned. Abnormality was suspect and this was abnormal. Common, but unusual.

"I'd better have a word with Benito," he said, and was agreeably surprised when Michael had the number of Benito's uncle's car rental company in North London. "And the girl," he said almost as an afterthought. "I suppose she has also come to London."

"As matter of fact, yes."

"I only deal in matters of fact," Bognor said humorlessly. "I leave conjecture to others." He almost said *foreigners* but checked himself. Dibdini was not English, but he was supposed to be a friend. Friendship came before nationality. Well, most of the time it did.

"They say all roads lead to Rome," said the Italian, "but in matters carnal, that is not evidently so. London is the center of the sexual universe."

"I thought she worked in a hotel," said Bognor, all faux-naif.

"That is what you might call a cover," said Dibdini. "In the hotel, the manager and the rest of the wigbigs turn the blind eye."

"Bigwigs," corrected Bognor, thinking to himself that the malapropism was more sonorous and actually better in most respects. "So she is a prostitute? Sophia?"

"Not at all," protested Dibdini, who clearly believed Bognor had maligned his alleged countrywoman. "She is what I believe you would describe as 'an enthusiastic amateur.' But if the gentleman is prepared to pay for her recreation, then she will take his money. And, forgive me, my friend, there are more men who will pay for pleasure in England than in Italy. In Italy, we do not believe that one should pay for pleasure."

"How can I find Sophia?" asked Bognor, and was unsurprised to be given the name of a well-known West End hotel. It was well known to those in his profession to be little more than what men of his class and generation described as a "knocking shop."

"So she's a tart masquerading as a washerwoman?"

"She is a maid who enjoys sex and uses her femininity to augment her wages," said Dibdini. It was his turn to sound pompous.

Bognor said he supposed he would have to talk to her, too, if only on the grounds of sexual equality. Privately, he did not see that an equation between sex and money made either person a murderer but if, on the other hand, one was prepared to sell one's body to any Tom, Dick, or Harry, you would presumably not flinch from being a hired assassin. He suddenly felt unaccountably weary.

"I'll let you know how I get on," he said. "For now, though, toodle pip." And he put down the receiver. He liked his telephones to be functional, traditional, and serviceable. Like sex. He sighed. If only life were not so complicated. So foreign. Much simpler to be British and to take one's pleasures seriously, even if they came at a price.

Bognor had no wish to have sex with Benito nor to be driven anywhere by him. He guessed that either would turn out to be something of a magical mystery tour and he had no wish to take such risks in matters sexual or transportational. He liked to know where he was going to end up in both instances and was too old for surprises. He did not, therefore, beat about the bush.

"I'm the head of SIDBOT," he said, "and I'm investigating the murder of Irving Silverburger. In Venice. During Carnival. When you were there."

"*Sì*," said Benito, "many people were there. And Signor Silverburger."

"Yes," said Bognor, sounding grim. "And you had sex with him?"

"*Sì*," he said.

"For money?"

"*Sì*," he repeated. He managed to imply that this was quite usual. Maybe it was.

"You also gondoliered him about the place."

"*Sì*," said the prostitutional oarsman. "That, too, was for money. Mr. Silverburger paid money."

"I put it to you," said Sir Simon, "that you killed Mr. Silverburger."

There was a silence. They were in the HQ of Benito's uncle's car rental company. The cars were all right, and the drivers, ditto, in a too-smooth-by-half, cavalier fashion. The latter spoke no known language and had only the shakiest knowledge of London. HQ, however, was terminally tacky with very ancient sofas, magazines of similar antiquity with such esoteric titles as *Practical Rollerskating*, and limited space. Clients never visited it. It existed only as a place for the drivers to rest between assignments. Clients would be put off. They liked their limos air-conditioned and leathery. HQ was a notch or three down and not designed for customers.

"Mr. Silverburger was killed?"

Simon could see that this was a question, but he was perplexed by it. Did it imply doubt about whether or not Silverburger was dead? Or that he was known to be dead, but doubt over whether or not he was murdered? And what, if anything, was the subtext? Was it a form of attack being the best defense? What exactly was it designed to suggest? Not for one moment did Bognor consider that it was anything as simple as an off-the-top-of-the-head spontaneous response to his question. Life was not like that. Sometimes he wished it was, but alas it was not as straightforward. There was no such thing as Q and A without a subtext.

These thoughts passed through Bognor's mind as he contemplated the apparently simple four words of Benito's question.

"Mr. Silverburger was killed."

This, too, was a gambit. The apparently simple four words said simply that Irving had been murdered by a person or persons unknown. Benito knew this. He also knew that Bognor knew he knew. This was a vital, if arcane, piece of knowledge, a little of which was dangerous. Seeing the whole picture was relatively safe, but only knowing one corner of the canvas was an invitation to conjecture and an admission of ignorance. The whole picture might be an icon, an impressionist, or a modern faux-naif à la Lowry. A small corner might provide a vital clue that led in the right direction. Or not.

Interviewing technique was interesting. He supposed he had evolved one, but basically he made it up as he went along and did not believe in rules. He did, however, believe in aphorisms and remembered the late Lord Chandos telling him once that the most significant conversational gambit in the English language was the grunt. This could mean whatever one wished depending on how one grunted. Enthusiasm conveyed approval. There was also the grunt dismissive, the grunt noncommittal, the grunt expecting the answer "yes"; ditto "no." It all depended on how you grunted. Evidently, it was not what you said, but how you said it. Oscar Wilde had something to say about style, not sincerity, being crucial in matters of great importance. This was one such occasion.

"He was shot in the back on his way to the airport in a motorboat. Someone was dressed in a costume. It was Carnival time so many people wore masks. Your colleague in Venice told me this, but it was not needed. Everyone in the city knew this. It was in the newspapers. On the radio and television. I was wearing a mask myself. I was driving the gondolier with the pole. It was impossible for me to kill Mr. Silverburger. Besides he was a customer. He paid much money and he made no complaint. I said this to your colleague in Venice."

"Of course," said Bognor. "You would hardly confess to

the crime even if you had committed it. Not the same as saying you're innocent."

Nor was it, Sir Simon thought. He sometimes wondered
if interrogations were worth it. Certainly, orthodox Q and
A sessions were suspect. If only lie detectors were reliable. It
was like Hawkeye, the electronic device that was supposed to
be infallible and that the Indians said was not able to make
reliable decisions with regard to leg before wicket. Bognor
thought that the Indians might have a point. However it was
more than his life was worth to say so in public. There would
be a chorus of dissent from the depths of armchairs. The
chorus would be muffled by a combination of sleep and *Daily
Telegraph*, but it would be nonetheless real.

"I did not kill Mr. Silverburger. He was my good friend."

"You would say that," countered the head of SIDBOT. "That
doesn't make either statement true or false. Just predictable."

The gondolier, turned taxi driver–male tart, who was
incapable of changing his spots, had the grace and self-
knowledge to hang his head. Bognor hoped it was shame
that made him do it.

"I would like to help," said Benito. "How can I help?
I would enjoy assisting you to find the person who killed
Irving. It was not . . . how do you say it? It was not necessary."

"No," he agreed. Privately, he thought that murder was
always a bit of a waste, but he did not feel that this was the
time for a philosophical discussion. Nor Benito the right person with whom to have one.

"Were you named after Mussolini?" he asked, and was

pleased to see the effect of this unusual form of questioning. At least there was some prospect of getting an honest response. It might even be revealing.

"My parents were both Fascists," Benito said without a moment's hesitation. "I, too, admire Il Duce. Mr. Silverburger, also. We have talked often about him."

Interesting. So Silverburger had been a Tea-Party man. A Neocon. Right wing. A Fascist. Benito likewise.

"My great-aunt was Rita Zucca. Great-Aunt Rita. Very fine lady. She lived to be very old. In an apartment in Mestre. Very old, but she had, how you say, spirit. She had a very fine spirit. My father, he drove a truck. He used to say that the *fascisti* built the *autostrada* and Il Duce made the trains punctual. In Britain, you need a good Fascist to build the new roads and organize the trains. You have not had such a person since Ernesto Marples. My father was a believer in Ernesto Marples." Benito pronounced the name Marples with a heavily accented final syllable whereas in English, the name had in effect only a single syllable with a sort of guttural plural on the end. The way Benito pronounced it made Ernest sound like a torero or indeed a friend of the Italian dictator. Bognor found it strange to think of Ernest Marples inspiring a cult following among Italian truck drivers, but there you went. Marples had been a flamboyant transport minister in a Conservative government when Bognor was growing up. Had he been Italian, thought Bognor, little Marples might have been a Fascist. But he was as British as a half of warm bitter, which meant he had to settle for a diluted form of conservatism. Bognor thought Ernest's prime minister was Harold Macmillan, who was many things but not a Fascist. Marples was responsible for introducing the seatbelt and Dr. Beeching, the scourge of the railways. He was also the founder of a construction company called Marples-Ridgway, which specialized in road building and represented a clear conflict of interest when Marples ran it while minister for transport. He spent the last few years of his life holed up in his chateau fleeing from the British tax authorities. He probably lacked the guts to be a fully fledged Fascist. He made, on Bognor's reflection, an improbable but plausible patron saint for Benito's truck-driving father and his great-aunt Rita who had, in her day, been a sort of Italian Lord Haw-Haw. She was in the habit of broadcasting anti-Allied propaganda during World War II, had been tried and sentenced to a prison term and subsequently vanished. Bognor occasionally and very idly wondered what had become of her. Now it transpired that she had lived to a ripe and spirited old age as well as being a fan of Ernest Marples.

Bognor shrugged and smiled. And now Benito. Ah, Benito.

"So you did not kill Irving Silverburger?" Bognor smiled a smile that was supposed to be feline. The words were the exact opposite to those he had uttered a few minutes earlier yet the sense of them was not so very different. This was the effect of inflection, the nature of the grunt, the triumph of style over substance.

"This is what I have said."

"You know Marshall McLuhan?" asked Bognor. "The medium, not the message. McLuhan is saying much the same as Wilde. It is not so much what purports to be said but the means of conveying it that makes the difference. Sometimes this affects the message itself. Do I make myself clear?"

Benito shook his head vigorously. Meaning and clarity were emphatically not what he was getting. "I am sorry," he said. "My English is not so good."

"I am sorry, also."

Pause. Not a long one, but sufficient for Bognor to use it to gather his thoughts. Eventually, he continued, "So on the one hand, you *did* shoot poor Silverburger, and on the other, you did not."

"No," said Benito. "I did not kill Irving. Not. Not. No. No. I did not kill him."

"Next thing I know, you'll be saying that I put words in your mouth. That's what most people say, especially when, like you, they don't speak much English. We have the same sort of problem with a great many natives. Just because you were born in England doesn't mean that you speak English. Not a problem I often encounter, but some of my colleagues, particularly in uniform, say they come across it most of the time. Well, maybe not *most*, but it's a worry, this Englishness of the non-practicing English person. We're not allowed to articulate it for fear of sounding racist, but it is a problem all the same."

He sighed. "Your English is not very good and you're not

very bright, so I can get you to say what I like. Or could if I were so inclined. Luckily for you, however, I am not a bent copper and I don't happen to believe you killed Silverburger."

"*Sì*," said Benito, nodding vigorously. "I mean, yes."

"Oxford Circus, Piccadilly Circus, Finsbury Circus. It's all the same thing. Bread for you, circuses for the punter. Same with airports—Heathrow, Gatwick, City, Southend, Stansted, Luton. They're all airports. Pays your money and you take your choice."

"You want to go to airport?" Benito asked eagerly. "You want fly? Foreign country. Aeroplane. Many, many *flap-flap*?"

Bognor sighed again.

"So you took Mr. Silverburger in your gondola. You quoted him a price. He paid. You took him to your bed. You mentioned money; named a figure. He paid. No love; no sense of occasion or direction. But it was commercial all around, and after you'd moored your boat and zipped up your flies, you simply said good-bye and never saw him again."

"Yes," said Benito. "Yes, yes. Irving Silverburger very nice man. He pay lot of money. Very correct. Not too much. Not too little. No rubber and bounce, bounce. Also please and thank you. Mr. Silverburger perfect gentleman. Perfect gentleman. You also?"

Bognor sighed for a third time and found himself wondering if this was significant. They said bad news came in threesomes; maybe it was true of sighs. He realized he could get a conviction easily.

Gondolier had sex with customer, then killed him. No

questions asked. Lover's tiff. Money and lust. Two perennial reasons for murder.

"You like to take people for a ride?" he asked rhetorically.

Benito smiled. "Of course," he said. "You like?"

"Not today, thanks," said Sir Simon. "I like to know where I'm going, so no rides today. Thanks all the same." He lied again. "You've been a great help," he said.

"No? No ride?" Benito seemed very disappointed. Crestfallen even. Though he wouldn't have understood.

16

The matter of M. Strauss-Kahn, the French head of the International Monetary Fund, accused of sexually assaulting a hotel maid but later released without trial, had dominated newspaper headlines for much of 2011. Newspapers had Mr. Murdoch and phone tapping, the Arab Spring, and much else to occupy themselves, but the *affaire* Strauss-Khan involved an allegedly libidinous Frog with presidential aspirations and a colored, relatively nubile female and was therefore grist to a particular old-fashioned hack and his equally old-fashioned mill. The fact that the story seemed to be all smoke and no fire was no bar to its headline quality, and the world thrilled accordingly.

French financiers of a certain age already enjoyed a dodgy reputation, but their attractive feminist wives came in for a bit of flak and the *affaire* did nothing for the already flaky reputation of female workers in the hotel industry. The fact that Irving Silverburger had enjoyed a commercially tainted fling with an employee of a Venetian hotel was in comparison a matter of little consequence.

American film producers, particularly of such quintessentially unintellectual appeal as *The Coffee Grinders*, were well known to drop their pants at anything that moved. Girls who worked in the hotel business were popularly supposed to be no better than they should be and would sell themselves short to anyone connected with film, even if the film were as ghastly as *The Coffee Grinders*.

"So," said Bognor, not beating about the bush, "you had sex with Mr. Silverburger and then shot him in the back with a crossbow. Bit extreme? Not up to much, was he?"

Sophia pouted. When she pouted, she looked sexy and Italian, which, for men such as Bognor, was the same, and meant Sophia Loren, Gina Lollobrigida, and Monica Vitti. Loren shared a Christian name with the hotel maid and had once enjoyed similarly pulchritudinous appeal. The three actresses were old maids or matrons now, even if still alive, but when Bognor and the world were young, they had been alluring, sexy, and inviting. The modern Sophia had a similar appeal, but Bognor was sort of past succumbing to it. Well, he was not, but he did not wish to appear ridiculous. Well, up to a point.

The modern Sophia spoke. "You think I'm stupid, don't you?"

Bognor considered this and eventually said that yes, on balance, he did.

"I have a degree in comparative biology from the University of Padua and an MBA from Harvard."

Inwardly, Bognor groaned. Outwardly, however, he smiled as if he had been expecting as much all along.

"So?" he said, showing his teeth.

"I am a graduate of a respectable university, and I have a master's in business administration from arguably the world's best."

"Even graduates from quite good universities are quite stupid," Bognor said drily. "Besides, I have never rated Harvard and, come to think of it, the same goes for courses in business studies."

"It is because I am a woman."

"On the contrary. Some of my best friends are women." He was thinking of Monica, aka Lady Bognor.

"Then why?"

"Even Apocrypha men can be stupid," Bognor said with feeling. "I don't think Oxford had anything to do with business until that ridiculous school with the foreign name. And that university you mention is just a Cambridge upstart on the wrong side of the Atlantic."

"I am an international courtesan," said Sophia, sounding fierce. "I charge in guineas and I accept plastic, especially pink."

"With respect," said Bognor, not giving any, "you're an

employee of a hotel. Quite a long way down the food chain, too. You clean and make beds."

"That is just a cover," she protested. "I am *une grande horizontale*. My credit score is fantastic. Better than yours."

"That's perfectly possible," agreed Bognor, who was not proud of his credit score on the grounds that he kept forgetting his password, did not appreciate the significance of his mother's maiden name, and was not much interested in finance in any case.

"My books are in order. In fact, they are matters of great beauty."

Bognor did not believe these sorts of books had the capacity for beauty. He had no respect for money, regarding it as a regrettable necessity and believing that there was much more to life.

"None of this has any relevance to the death of Silverburger," he said.

"I take American Express and Diners," said Sophia, eyes flashing. "I am not merely a common garden maid. I am a professional and I am a graduate."

"Yes, well," said Bognor, having his doubts about the universities in question and about Sophia's presence there. She had probably made beds in both places, and in more senses than one. She may or may not have been clever or well qualified, but she was certainly sexy.

"So Mr. Silverburger paid you for sex?"

"He paid for my companionship. Anything more was private." For the first time, she dimpled. Prettily. Bognor was intrigued. He would never have followed the deceased as far as Benito was concerned, but the courtesan was another matter.

He remembered how on one occasion after the two men had had a drink at some conference, Parkinson had asked what Bognor "did" about sex, adding the implausible but very British rider that it's hardly the sort of thing that one can discuss with one's wife. Bognor reflected that one's wife was precisely the sort of person with whom one had to discuss sexual matters, but then, he supposed, not for the first time, that he was different. Monica even more so.

"I don't see that your academic qualifications or your financial probity have anything to do with the deceased's demise," he said pompously.

"You think that because I'm a girl and work in hotels and enjoy men and sex that makes me automatically stupid. And also you think that a stupid, sexy woman who works in a hotel is easy meat. You may think I killed Silverburger, but that is really immaterial. You could pin it on me because most people, especially male, think I'm a low form of life. As such, they reckon I could have killed Mr. Silverburger. The only real reservation is that it's unlikely that a woman could shoot straight."

"Well, you said it," agreed Sir Simon. "I don't believe women can drive cars. And, certainly, they can't park or read a map the right way up. Or shoot straight. They are only any good cooking or making love. That's what men think. According to the stereotype. If you believe that all men behave in a certain way and all women in another, then that's what you'll believe. I happen to think life is more complicated than that; but then, I'm old-fashioned."

Sophia seemed reassured by this. She relaxed. Or gave the impression of doing so.

"You seem to conform to a type," she said, "but something about you suggests otherwise. Are you a Pisces?"

"I'm flattered," said Bognor, who was. "And I haven't the foggiest notion if I am a Pisces or not. I don't believe in signs. I'm resolutely opposed to such things." He really did not and he really was. Queer fellow, Bognor. Very.

"This doesn't help me resolve the question of who killed Irving Silverburger," he said. "Was it you?"

She pouted and said *pouf*, or words to that effect. She would, wouldn't she? But Bognor was inclined to believe her. He recognized that he was a victim of prejudice. He could see that he was prejudiced against women in a general, and therefore sexist, way. He was prejudiced against the hotel industry, particularly those who worked in a menial capacity. This was, presumably snobbery. And was prejudiced against those who sold sex for money. This had presumably been dinned into him as a form of puritanism having its origins in a particular sort of regimented religion. This, too, was prejudice. On the one hand, recognition was one thing, doing anything about it quite another. He was a creature of prejudice and he knew it. However, he accepted it. It was the way he was made. Possibly, this was regrettable, but it was also necessary. Perhaps this was why the regrettable necessity had entered the language and become a cliché.

In any event, he conceded that he suspected Sophia for a number of reasons, most of them reprehensible. There was no reason for believing that she had killed Silverburger any more than his accountant, his catamite, or his confessor. Bognor had been taught to *cherchez la femme* and if she was a hotel maid and a bit of a trollop, then she deserved everything she got. She did not, of course, but only Germaine Greer would have proclaimed her innocence. Well, young Germaine; old Germaine would have led the stone throwers. But that, too, was prejudice. It wasn't Greer's fault that she had once written that book and appeared to change sides in old age. She was Australian. Oh God, he must stop making up his mind prematurely and on no evidence. Some of his best friends . . .

Out loud, he said, "You must admit, though . . ."

"I'm admitting nothing."

Bognor began to suspect that the girl was right about university even if Harvard was a claim too far. But did academic qualifications, real or imaginary, make Sophia a murderer? Did being a hotel maid? Or a prostitute? Or just female? He sighed.

"Very droll," he said. "In some countries, your behavior would be criminal."

"Not where I come from."

"Which is?" he asked nonchalantly.

"Let's just say that I am a citizen of the world. I mean a

girl has to live and I enjoy my job. I like men. I enjoy giving pleasure. Sometimes I take a little myself." She smiled.

"And money?" he said. "You always take money?"

"Not always," she said. "But basically, I'm a professional person and I charge for my services. Everything is explicitly stated in black and white, and I always keep my side of the bargain."

"And Mr. Silverburger?"

"Very straight. I got the impression he'd done it before. Paid cash in a plain envelope. No frills. Straightforward. Bit of unprotected *soixante-neuf*, which I happen to be rather good at. Then he took me in a doggy position, which we both enjoyed. He stayed an hour."

"Too much information," said Bognor, embarrassed. She smiled archly.

"Anyone would think," she said. "But then men are basically all the same. You wouldn't be coy for long."

"And did you talk? Or rather listen? Did Mr. Silverburger have anything interesting to say?"

"He was quite British in an American way," she said. "He talked about the weather. And sex, of course. He was bisexual. Made no excuses. He was quite frank. Just enjoyed himself. He was complimentary about Italians. And about Venice. He liked Venice—went on about Harry's Bar and gondoliers. I think he saw himself as a bit of a Hemingway. He was about delusions, thought he was owed a living, seemed aggrieved with the world. That was my impression. I felt a bit sorry for him."

"Was he . . . I mean did he . . . ?"

She laughed and helped him out.

"He was all right for a man of his age. Went through the right motions. I didn't get the impression that it was a first time. I felt he was into being professional and commercial. Suited me. He was okay, clean, polite, but he treated the whole exercise as a job, something he had to do, get out of the way. I'd say he was perfunctory. He never felt as if he was enjoying himself. Not like some of my clients. He was a quick, efficient, soulless sort of an individual. Not like some. I quite like that. Maybe he had a physical need. I couldn't say."

"But you said he was into illusion."

"Not about sex. I mean, I have a number of outfits. I am quite adroit when it comes to role-playing. A lot of men like to be dominated. I have whips, handcuffs, uniforms, but he didn't seem to want anything like that. Just straightforward. Makes quite a difference, I can tell you."

"So you felt he was suffering from delusions about himself? Nothing to do with sex?"

"Everything is to do with sex. Deep down. But superficially, Irving was about *crash, bang,* thank you, ma'am. Complicated, yes; but that took the form of being straight and simple when it came to sex. By the way, I enjoy what I do; I am independent not exploited. But if I don't work, I don't get paid. So if you have no more questions, I have to earn a crust. You know where to find me. And Irving was a regular guy and a perfect punter. I'm sorry he's dead. Really. But life goes on. And some of us have to work."

Whereupon she gave Bognor a perfunctory peck of a kiss.

"And," she said, leaving with no excuses, "if you want a massage, you know where to go. No deals, but the price structure is set out in black and white. As Mr. Silverburger knew. He was a gent. Daresay, you are, too."

He said as little as possible to Monica about Sophia and not a lot more about Benito. This was for no very good reason. He simply judged it sensible. His wife was wise in the ways of the world, rather wiser than he himself, but he still thought it better to say nothing about Sophia. One did not discuss such things as sex with one's partner however much one loved her. It would have been bad form. Like discussing money. The fact that so many other people did so was all the more reason. Other people were, in his experience, usually wrong. It had something to do with other people being other people.

Besides Monica disapproved of what David Holbrook described as "the commodification of sex." So did Bognor, but he was a great believer in respecting other people's point of view and their right to an opinion. Besides, he thought of Sophia as a human being and not a commodity. Nor did he consider her exploited. He suspected his wife would disagree with him about many of these things, and he was not in the mood for disagreement. Seldom, if ever, was. Particularly, with Monica.

"Good day?" she wanted to know, to which he replied as he so often did that it had been comme ci, comme ça. The Bognors were conducting their habitual postmortem over an early evening cocktail, as was their custom. They had been doing this for years, evidence once more of their age and class.

"Any news on the Silverburger case?" asked Lady Bognor.

Bognor ruminated visibly and finally said, "Loads of interviews. No real developments."

"If I may say so, that is the story of your life. What's more, this case is fairly typical, too. Nasty piece of work is bumped off by an ingenious killer who has done us all a service."

"Killing people is wrong," said her husband. "It doesn't make the slightest difference if the world is better off without the stiff nor if the crime is clever. Justice must be done. This is where I come in. I solve crimes indiscriminately because it is my belief that a crime is a crime is a crime."

"That's just pompous claptrap," said Lady Bognor, ameliorating the sting in the words with a smile. The smile was horribly sardonic and Sir Simon noticed. It was not a thing of mirth.

"That's what you always say," he said, "but you will agree that we can't go taking the law into our own hands much as we might like to. The more popular a crime, the more important is my involvement. Any Tom, Dick, or Harry can detect a nasty murderer who kills someone horrid. It takes someone like me to find nice murderers who have done in someone we all dislike. But it has to be done. This is what makes for a civilized society. It's one of the things that distinguishes men from animals."

"Now you're really sounding pompous," she said, "and you don't believe it. You think Silverburger deserved it and you rather applaud the Harlequin with the crossbow."

"My personal feelings have nothing to do with individual cases. There is an important principle involved. Justice has to be served. Justice is blind. Rightly so. Me, too."

He hated seeming pompous. Being right so often did; being wrong was much more attractive and human.

"Someone once said that the perfect crime was pushing one's partner off Beachy Head. That was the perfect murder," Monica said thoughtfully. "Seems to me that shooting a traveler in a boat in the back with a crossbow while dressed as Harlequin in the middle of the Venetian Carnival is just as good. Undetectable. It's down to an obvious motive and a proper confession. Have you considered torture?"

"We don't do torture."

Monica made a show of appearing to choke on her scotch.

"Don't be so naive," she said. "Who doesn't do torture? The Brits? The Board of Trade?"

"We don't do torture. I don't do torture. I never beat anyone at school when I was a prefect. I don't believe in such things. Also I think torture and beating are counterproductive." He was aware that he was sounding prim. Too bad. He knew he was right.

"Oh, grow up," she said testily. "Torture is a fact of life. Everyone does it. We want results; we have to live. Even stiff upper-lip Brits do it. You know the sort of thing; 'this is going to hurt me more than it hurts you.' It's the perennial British preamble to six of the best. You must have heard that at school."

"Not from me," said Bognor. "I don't do that sort of

thing. Only savages do. We are not animals. There is a difference. And what are we fighting for if we behave like that? Besides which, I have always had a contempt for the argument that says that everyone else is doing it, so why not me. Next thing we'll be saying that we are only carrying out orders. It's a Fascist argument and that is one thing I'm not."

His voice was rising. The octave count was dangerously high.

"You might have been a Turk or dirty Russian, a Dago, Wop, or Prussian, but instead you are an Englishman." Lady Bognor set these words to her idea of music though Sir Arthur Sullivan would not have recognized the noise. Nor W. S. Gilbert, the words. Never mind, the sentiments were clear.

"Now you're being silly."

An outsider would have said they were arguing and maybe they were. On the other hand, they had always behaved like this and they were still together after all these years. Bickering was part of marital life. Strife was endemic and just another word for love. That at least was the theory. Third parties were often appalled, but they were, well, third parties. What did they really know? Even close friends and relatives asked whether they always bickered thus, and the answer was always yes and invariably meant that they provided a united front against anyone who suggested otherwise.

Some people did not take their arguments seriously, a confusion that arose from a failure to distinguish between facetious style and facetious content. It was possible to be deadly earnest while appearing to be determinedly insouciant. This was not always appreciated by the second-rate, seldom by the third, and never by the fourth or below. A. L. Rowse would have appreciated the distinctions, but few others. Most people confused seriousness with solemnity and believed that in order to be taken without a pinch of salt, one had to eschew seasoning altogether. A smile was nearly always playing around Bognor's lips, but only a fool would dismiss him as a mere comedian. Luckily for him, there were a great many fools around.

"Don't you call me silly," said Lady Bognor. "You don't have to be a Lancastrian infantryman to enjoy beating people up. Some fastidious first-class minds have been more than happy to use the results obtained by unscrupulous methods about which they profess ignorance. Hypocrisy is almost as prevalent as torture, and they tend to accompany each other. The really effective torturer is the one who wrings his hands. And pretends to disapprove."

"You know what?" Bognor was adroit at a sudden change of subject when it suited him. Now was just such a moment.

"What?" Lady Bognor was a willing party to the obvious subterfuge.

"You know that last scene in a dame-written who-dunnit? The one in the library when the sleuth reveals all, via a number of red herrings until he tells everyone who the culprit is? Whereupon the guilty party pulls a gun and is overpowered before going off to face a hanging judge armed with the full panoply of the law and a black cap, which he wears to pronounce sentence."

"Which is always that the guilty party be taken from this place and hanged by the neck."

"I suppose so, yes."

"Well"—his wife spoke as if this settled an old argument beyond reasonable doubt—"I hate to tell you this, but the days of capital punishment are long gone. Judges sentence, but not to death. We don't kill people. Not on legalized gibbets. We don't hang people by the neck anymore."

"That doesn't rule out the final scene in the library."

"It makes it much less final," she said, sounding like someone whose mind was made up. "Like a funeral without a box and a body. Not the same thing at all. I loathe memorial services for that reason. Give me coffins, veils, and tears."

"I've always slightly hankered after a denouement in a library."

"Well, you can have one, but it won't be the same without the ultimate sanction. Same with crime, generally. It's not the same without legal killing. That's a real do-as-you-would-be-done-by situation. Modern life has bowdlerized murder. Life imprisonment isn't the same. Besides, it only rarely means life."

"I still fancy that scene."

She shrugged. "It involves omniscience. The detective has to know everything. He is privy to all thoughts, knows all the motives, understands every clue. He is never baffled. You, on the other hand, live in a state of constant bafflement, see every side of every argument. It's infuriating, but lovable. It's why I married you."

"If the detective is male, he smokes a pipe. Mine's a meerschaum. Maybe female sleuths smoke pipes, too. Did Miss Marple smoke a pipe?"

"In the Margaret Rutherford incarnation possibly. But Dame A. would not have approved. She was definitely anti-smoking."

"Oh, I don't know," said Bognor. "Poirot smoked."

"Did he? David Suchet smokes on telly when he plays Poirot, but I'm not sure the real character does so on the page. The dame wouldn't have known one end of a cigarette from the other."

"Cigarettes are like that. Unless, of course, they are filtered. One end of an unfiltered fag is much like the other. Cigarettes don't have a business end and an exhaust until one actually starts smoking. So the dame wasn't being ignorant, just rational. She usually was. It's her critics who are ignorant."

"Yes. Well." Monica certainly wasn't going to admit defeat. Instead, she changed tack. "Seems to me you're further than ever from finding Silverburger's killer," she said.

"We have a list of suspects," said Bognor, taking mild umbrage, "and I have interviewed them."

"Precisely," said his wife. "The list consists of people who knew Irving and were in Venice at the time. You've talked to them, but you've established less than nothing. You have absolutely no idea who shot the bolt. Not the foggiest. Given the circumstances, that's probably not surprising. It sounds like the perfect murder. Everyone was in disguise. No one knew or cared who anyone else really was. *Perfetto.*"

"I wouldn't say that," said Bognor, still huffy. "Dibdini and I have narrowed it down. We have a list."

"Your list is worthless and you know it. It could have been anyone. Disguise was universal, and no one knew he had been murdered until the crime had been committed and the deceased and the murderer were miles away from each other. Literally. I don't see how you can reasonably expect to solve this one. And why, anyway? The world is obviously better off without him. It's the perfect crime and like so many perfect crimes, not only faultless in execution, timing and what-have-you, but also in the choice of victim. No one liked him and the world is a better place without him. Better stick to bowling."

"I don't bowl," he said, "as you well know. I agree that the crime looks perfect, but that's an illusion. There's no such thing as the perfect crime any more than there is a perfect anything—rice pudding, shot at goal, after-dinner speech."

"Oh, I don't know." She seemed to be thinking about the notion as if it were new.

"Well, I do," said Bognor. "Perfection is a chimera. It doesn't exist. The huge advantage of this is that so many people believe it to be true. In fact, there is always a flaw, a chink, a downright mistake. And that is our strength. This murderer believes he has committed the perfect crime. That is his great weakness. Akin to believing your own publicity."

"You're trying to lull him or her into a false sense of security. Incidentally, why does the notion of security always carry an aura of falseness?"

"Because, darling, security is always false. There is no such thing as security and the more pride and sense of security, the greater the fall. The ancients knew a thing or two."

"So you think the killer may become overconfident and give you the equivalent of a gift?"

"I'm certain," said Bognor, "which is why I am going to treat myself to the luxury of a denouement in the library. I think this calls for luncheon. I will summon all suspects to luncheon in the club. There all will be revealed. Feel free to come along and learn the identity of the person who fired a bolt from the Bridge of Sighs during Carnival."

"Thanks," said Monica. "I will."

17

The club (aka "The Club") was as much of a pastiche as the denouement. Both were artificial inventions, imitations of the real thing. Had Bognor been in a position to pocryphize Whites, Boodles, or that club on the other side of the street whose name he could never quite remember, he would have come up with something more or less like The Club. It was not the real thing, although in some ways it was an improvement. The food, for instance. They still specialized in variations on meat and suet puddings, but they did not overboil the cabbage; the jam roly-poly was really rolled and contained real jam; and, generally speaking, although recognizably clublike, the scoff was edible. Not like the real thing, which reminded members of days that in a gastronomic sense were quite definitely not the happiest of their lives.

Bognor hired the library, which was appropriate and typical. The books had been ordered by the yard, and they were unread. Indeed, you could not read them because they were the bibliophilic equivalent of skin deep, having no printed pages but beautifully bound. The binding was literally everything, for it was antique leather and it smelled similar—in other words of elderly goat. The books ran all around the room; it was much like a ducal library, especially in so far as the average English duke was not much into actual reading. Your average English duke enjoyed boasting that he had never read a book unless you counted a volume or so of P. G. Wodehouse, who was the only English author of whom the duke basically approved.

Bognor sighed. He was, he knew, insufficiently grand and perhaps stuffy for Whites, Boodles, or the service clubs. The converse was true of places such as the Groucho. Perhaps he was just unclubbable. On the other hand, he had a yearning for leathery armchairs, other people, and even port. Hence, he supposed, The Club, of which he was a founding member. This was fortuitous. He had had a letter suggesting funding; an aunt had recently died leaving a modest legacy. He had no money to burn but a small amount to squander. As a consequence, he had invested in The Club in the eighties when it was clear that he and Monica were destined to be childless.

In a way and up to a point, he enjoyed it. It was an escape, and he knew no other members. He liked the staff and the food and the anonymity. It was also a good place in which to entertain, and even cabinet ministers were pleased and flattered to be invited there. Essentially, it was a club for the unclubby, and he identified with this aim. He liked to think of himself as beyond (enemies would insist on beneath) classification. He did not belong and never would, but this did not prevent him from hankering after some of the concomitants of playing for a team. Loners were like that. Just because you walked alone, did not mean that you enjoyed the sensation.

Irving Silverburger had not been a member of The Club. In a number of important respects, he was perfect membership material, but he lacked one important qualification: he was not popular. He was natural blackball material, and someone would have destroyed any prospect of election. In this sense, The Club was like any other. Aspiring members required a proposer and a seconder. Their names were placed in a book, and members were invited to indicate their approval with a signature. From time to time, members were blackballed, which is to say that members objected to their election. One voice was enough to sustain non-election. And though you could bet that normally apathy would prevent such an occurrence, you would put your money on one or two members doing so in the unlikely event that Silverburger would find anyone foolish enough to propose and second him.

So there were no Silverburgers in The Club. It was central,

comfortable; the food and drink were easy on the stomach, and the largely female staff was easy on the eye and affable. Bognor had always wanted a usual table, and at The Club he had one. Membership was an indulgence, an extravagance, but, crucially, Monica allowed it.

The other members were loners like Bognor. They were essentially unclubbable and not team players. This did not make them selfish or antisocial, but they were notably deficient in what Bognor thought of as "herd instinct" and they were high on an individuality, which he prized. They couldn't, however, have been as individual as they thought or they would not, like him, have enjoyed The Club as much as he did. And this was the point. It was not so much that Bognor and other members of The Club did not like the idea, more that there had hitherto been no club for the likes of them. Now there was.

So The Club existed for those for whom there had previously been no such animal. Mr. Silverburger was emphatically not a member, nor were any of those suspected of killing him. The suspects were, however, pleased to be asked. Obviously, no one had told them that food and drink did not come free. If they had told them, the suspects presumably felt that they were exceptions to this rule. If it were a rule, they would prove exceptions or even overturn it altogether. The suspects were nothing if not confident.

Bognor ran through them in his head. The first was Eric Swanley, né Braun. It was not Eric's fault that he was an accountant. Nor that he was originally German. It was more indicative of the sort of person that Bognor was that he had a prejudice against both. He disliked accountants because they were on the side of money, authority, neatness, and tidiness and he, personally, was against all of these. Not violently so, but he could see no point in them. He had the salaried person's secure contempt for wealth and the greed that, in his opinion, was its natural concomitant. He was not naturally neat and he had never been any good at arithmetic, not basically seeing the point of sums. As for Germans, it was all to do with the war and football. He recognized that this was ridiculous, but he could not help himself. He had no aversions to foreigners in general, or to Germans when encountered in real life, but in the abstract he disliked the idea. Some of his best friends were German accountants, but he convinced himself that they were exceptions and proved nothing.

He tended to think of accountants as "bean counters" and Germans as Krauts. The combination was lethal, and from time to time he could be heard sounding off to Monica or even Harvey Contractor about "Kraut bean-counters," than whom there were few things worse. On the other hand calling people "Kraut bean-counters" did not mean you thought of German accountants in that way. It was a variation of calling a spade a spade and came into the same category as the duke of Edinburgh's strictures on the Chinese and Indians. Just because Prince Philip was on record as saying that Chinese were slitty-eyed or Indian wiring was a shambles, did not mean he was prejudiced. To believe so was a failure to understand the nature of prejudice.

So, Eric Swanley seemed a typical English accountant from suburban Kent, but he was actually a Kraut bean-counter from the former Communist East. Leipzig, probably. The fact that he was German; that his real name was Braun was no more important than his profession but the deception mattered. The deceit was significant. Lie about one thing and you might lie about another. You became a liar and the truth was of diminished value. Eric Swanley was a liar. This did not make him better or worse as a person, but it meant that where crime was concerned he was always a suspect. Bognor, rightly or wrongly, believed that men such as Swanley had difficulty telling the truth. He believed that the Swanleys were part of life's majority. This was not helpful but it was what he believed, and it did not make his life any easier. Yet if he disliked Swanley, which on the whole he did, it was not because of his attitude to the truth. On the contrary, it made Swanley interesting, which in many respects he was not.

Bognor smiled. He recognized that he admired consistency more than rectitude. It didn't matter whether one was bad or good, the important thing was that one should always be one or the other. It made his job easier, of course, but that was not really the point. Like many who regarded life as a game and their part in it as entertainment and not to be taken too seriously, he relished a genuine struggle. He did not appreciate the theft of confectionery from small children and much preferred a contest with someone of more or less equal strength.

He supposed Eric S. came into this category, but he was

not disposed to think of him as an equal. He struck Bognor as quintessentially gray, which was an aged insult from his days at university. Many perfectly acceptable people were designated as "that little gray man from . . ." You filled in the name of the gray man's college with a sneer, which was universally mandatory, for the verdict had been issued with a truculence common to Apocrypha men who believed themselves to be at least a cut above all aspiring rivals. Membership of another college was just part of the grayness and inferiority.

Prejudice was a vital component in anyone's makeup, but it must not interfere with one's professionalism. That meant recognizing it and keeping it out of the way. It was folly to pretend it did not exist but that was very far from implying that one had to succumb to it. Rationality was what distinguished man from animals. The ability to think was vital. Thinking straight was probably a different matter and implied a rare triumph of the mind, but one had to aspire to such a state. That was what made a great detective.

Not that Sir Simon thought of himself as a "great" detective. Good, yes. Unusual and unorthodox. But of course. Great was probably not part of his vocabulary, certainly not as far as detection went, for the concept smacked of hero worship, which was definitely not his style. He was not so much egalitarian as insufferable where fools were concerned. In other words, he believed that he was as good as anyone now in practice. That did not mean "great" because greatness was not thrust upon anyone who was top of the batting averages. "Greatness" only came along once in every generation or so. It had to be earned and the idea had been abused. He was elitist; he set high, almost Rowseian standards. This meant that he regarded himself as at the top of his tree, but that tree was a mere sapling compared with greatness that sat at the top of the equivalent of a redwood.

He smiled once more. It was just one reason that he enjoyed the old-fashioned book. One could turn the pages, aimlessly flitting about in a seemingly purposeless way just as he had been. One could open something old-fashioned and encyclopaedic such as *Brewer's Dictionary of Phrase and Fable* at random, then just a few minutes later after a haphazard and apparently aimless riffling of paper one ended far from the original intention. Books were voyages of discovery, and one had no idea where they might lead.

The Internet and new technology were a quest for knowledge and information, which led in predictable directions. On the Net, one ended at a predictable destination. The old-fashioned book led in a series of more or less random directions. Two people could start at the same beginning and travel to different destinations. That was one of the factors that gave old-fashioned books their appeal.

It was musing such as this that made him so maddening to so many others. He must return to the matter in hand; *revenez aux moutons.* Swanley, Eric. He did not like the idea of Swanley for a number of reasons, which had nothing to do with Mr. Silverburger or his murder. With regard to that, his inclination was to give Mr. Swanley or whoever he was the benefit of whatever doubt he might be harboring. On the other hand, he could not eliminate him altogether for he was in Venice at the time of the murder and he knew the dead man. The fact that he had no discernible motive was probably neither here nor there.

Bognor sighed. *Next up*, he said to himself.

Trevor was the second suspect. He, like Swanley, was not what he seemed. To the uninitiated or gullible, he seemed just an English manservant, a gentleman's gentleman who did. Quite what he did was anyone's guess, but this was often the case with manservants. There was no universal job description.

But Trevor was a Balt, and Trevor was not his real name. That did not make him a criminal, much less a murderer, but it did mean that "Trevor" was a liar and that his identity was false. Such subterfuge was understandable, and there was a sense in which one was able in a free society to be whoever one liked. Even so the manservant was not whom he originally was. He was christened Artis, his surname was Dombrovskis, which may or not have given him a political dimension, and he was not high on the list of Contractor's list of suspects, which may have been why the interview with him at Silverburger's funeral had been perfunctory and non-revealing. Contractor's hunches were just that—hunches, no more and no less. The fact that they were more often right than not was coincidental though compelling. There was no scientific or forensic basis for Contractor's accuracy but, even though irrational, it was worth following Contractor's nose.

Bognor thought that Trevor modeled himself on Laurence Harvey who came from Lithuania but was the most famous Balt actor, notoriously bisexual and assumed the name Harvey either from the Harvey Nichols department store or the Bristol wine company that was synonymous with cream sherry. Harvey worked for Frank Sinatra, was romantically entangled with the actress Hermione Gingold (who was old enough to be his mother) and was widely said to have the morals of an alley cat though the judgment was thought to be unfair on urban felines. Trevor came from suburban Riga and had a sexy walk-on part in *The Coffee Grinders* though he claimed to have met Irving G. later.

Bognor had decided that this particular deception was something to do with visas or at worst show biz. That did not mean that Trevor was nice. On the contrary, he was an obvious no-good who could not even act or sneer as well as Harvey. He was keen to get out of his particular Baltic state and he was prepared for whatever stratagem was needed and, if that meant lies and Silverburger, it meant lies and Silverburger. Besides, it dented what little motive he might have had. As with so many of the "suspects," the deceased was more value to him alive than dead. He might have been a lousy film director and a rotten human being, but he was a benefactor of sorts even if he dealt mainly in plastic and pink plastic at that.

Trevor had lied in order to get out of Latvia. He had lied about Silverburger. He had lied about *The Coffee Grinders*. Trevor was all lies, but he was largely a creation of the late Irving and he owed his continued existence to him, too. In other words, Trevor may have been a bad hat, but he had a vested interest in keeping Silverburger alive and, for that matter, sweet. So Swanley and Trevor could have committed the crime on the grounds that they were in Venice at the time of death, and they were easily bad enough. On the other hand, they were better off with Silverburger alive. There was no reason for either man killing him. Rather the reverse.

Bognor swore lightly. Two down and no obvious killer. Ingrid Vincent, the faded starlet, was perhaps more plausible on the grounds that Silverburger might not have given her work in his new film. On the other hand, Silverburger was more likely to give her work than anyone else. He had at least heard of her and had indeed given her work. Alas, her salad days were behind her, and she relied more than most women on pulchritudinous looks, which tended to go with a certain age. It could not be said that she had weathered well or grown into anything. If she were a weather forecaster on TV, she would have been put out to grass long before. Perhaps one should not say such things, but Bognor believed in honesty.

It was more than likely that Silverburger would not have cast her in his long-awaited sequel to *The Coffee Grinders* and yet, without him, the probability of an enforced retirement became a certainty. Irving represented a slim hope, but it was a hope of sorts. If his diagnosis were correct, then Ingrid was also in the clear. She, too, was not what she seemed, and her life was founded on a lie. But whose wasn't? Bognor supposed that the alleged friends of Irving G. Silverburger were more than usually duplicitous, but he was reluctant to cast stones.

Bognor believed that most people's lives were founded on deception. But then he was straying into fields philosophical. What, after all, was identity? Did age matter? Or sex, come to that? Was Ingrid Vincent doomed because so much of her career depended on her appearance? Did she not have a personality? Did she not bleed? Oh God.

Bognor went to the window of his office and looked down at the populace scurrying hither and yon. Had not the duke of Wellington once liked to sit in the window of Brook's Club, praying for rain in order that he could watch the "damn people get wet?" Was this relevant or just a red herring? Was there a problem with the irrelevant? Bognor had a soft spot for things that seemed at first to be irrelevant for they had the knack, in his experience, of fitting what he saw as life's jig saw. There was a logic to life, though determining what that logic was, was given to very few. Those who could detect patterns to existence were either geniuses or morons. You had to be very stupid or incredibly bright to discern the meaning of life and Bognor was neither. Appreciating this was what lifted him out of the rut and made him different.

So Ingrid Vincent was more of a suspect than Swanley or Trevor but not by much. The first two were definitely better off with Silverburger alive, and Ingrid Vincent probably came into the same category. She might have harbored a grudge about becoming older and losing her looks, but Irving would hardly have been so tactless as to remind her of the passing of time and the consequent of history. Ye who are left grow old. Something like that. It appeared to be worse for women and particularly so for those who in their youth had traded on their looks. Even Ingrid could hardly have blamed Irving Silverburger for this, and he had given her a break of sorts. On the other hand, Ingrid was very stupid and Irving, particularly when provoked, could seem gratuitously rude.

He decided to move on, leaving La Vincent with a penciled "Not Guilty" rather than an inked one. Sophia and Benito were different. They were sexual mercenaries, and Silverburger had paid his bills and, within strange limits, behaved like an officer and a gentleman. The girl and the gondolier had both been in Venice at the time of death, and the nature of their work made both, in Bognor's book, suspicious.

This, too, was prejudice. He knew it and he was ashamed. But nevertheless, it existed, and to pretend otherwise was counterproductive. He knew that selling one's body for sex carried no baggage and was perfectly legal in many enlightened countries. However, he had been brought up in a world that believed, sort of, that the body was a temple and not to be defiled by acts of prostitution. Or that was what his society purported to believe. It was also endemically hypocritical, which was a different sort of problem but probably more real than the original proposition. Prostitution is wrong, but given certain circumstances, we sleep with the practitioners. We don't publicly approve of sex, but privately we get up to all sorts of tricks. Something like that.

One had to accept that most men were simply the sum of their prejudices. What mattered more than the prejudices themselves was the way in which one dealt with them. Bognor's way, which he obviously believed to be correct, was to acknowledge their existence but to put them to one side. Bearing this in mind, he considered the two professionals.

The girl, Sophia, was Russian by origin, cosmopolitan in fact and she worked in a hotel. This was a front and acknowledged as such. Working in hotels brought her into contact with men who were as often as not deprived of female companionship but also often craved it. They tended to be lonely and quite often they were drunk. These two facts of male hotel-life made the places lucrative hunting grounds for women like Sophia. Ingrid Vincent should have tried. Maybe she had, though Bognor dismissed the thought as soon as it first occurred. He had no evidence and was simply succumbing to the prejudice, which—untrammeled—could have interfered with his professionalism.

This was the nature of Sophia's relationship with the dead man. Under normal circumstances, the sex act would have carried all kinds of emotional undertones involving emotion, feeling, even love. This, however, was not like that. It was a professional assignment: *wham, bam*, thank you, ma'am. You paid your money and . . . Bognor wondered how many such tricks Sophia turned in a single day. And whether she took plastic. Or pink. It did not matter. All that mattered was that there was no likelihood of a motive either way. Sophia would erase Silverburger from her mind once the act was over. She probably did not consider him as a human being even when the act was taking place. That was probably the only way in which she could navigate through life. Whether or not she was a graduate of Harvard, she was plainly intelligent and educated. He had half a mind to consider her sensitive, but—given the nature of her calling—this was probably a stretch. Bognor found the pragmatic approach to sex alien to what he and Monica got up to, but he was man enough to recognize that theirs was not the only way.

The same could be said for Benito, the gondolier/taxi driver. As far as he was concerned, sex was a job, was a job, was a job. The chances of him remembering Silverburger, let alone killing him, were negligible. It was just as likely that he would be able to recall details of who precisely he had had in the back of his cab or the stern of his boat. In fact, if Irving were a celebrity, Benito would be much more likely to remember him in the back of his cab than the depths of his bed. Such was a taxi driver's stock-in-trade.

Once more, Sir Simon sighed. He could not, in all conscience, claim that either Sophia or Benito had a motive. As far as they were concerned, Irving Silverburger was just another trick or John. Bognor could not get into the mind of either the maid or the gondolier. To be honest, he had no wish to do so. Like so many others both on and off his little list, both of them had the opportunity. They were in Venice on the day of his departure, but they had no more motive than Swanley, Trevor, or Ingrid. This was tiresome but true.

Both had known Silverburger. And what is more, they

had done so in a biblical sense, but this meant very little, if anything. If either had enjoyed anything approaching an *affaire*, that would have been different, but they had not. Instead, theirs had been a commercial arrangement, pure and simple. Well, maybe not so pure but straightforward and of no significance. Yes, they had both known the dead man, but they had done so fleetingly, taken his money, smiled, bared all, dressed, and departed. All this was in a day's work. It should not have been so but, alas, it was.

Alas, poor Silverburger.

18

Bognor had always wanted a classic denouement in the library with him playing an omniscient God and disconcerting all the suspects with his fiendishly clever solution. More to the point, this author has always hankered after such a scene; wherein lies a problem, which is one of author involvement and reader awareness. Generally speaking, it is not considered proper for the author to interfere in a work of fiction. I suppose it destroys the essential delusion. I mean everyone knows who the author is, but the conceit is that he or she has to appear anonymous and to pretend that the characters have lives of their own and do as they please.

Anyone who has ever written a book knows that there is some truth in this. Sir Simon Bognor is a case in point. He was invented by an author and is inclined to do what the author tells him to, but not always. From time to time, punters furrow their brows and ask whatever happened to that character of mine, "Bugger" or "Weymouth"—they invariably get his name wrong. From time to time, they want to know where he went to school or what food or drink he prefers. Sometimes I know; sometimes I feel I should and bluff; and occasionally, I say I do not know but will ask next time I see him.

Much like any old friend.

Mr. and Mrs. Swanley arrived first and each chose an orange juice after a thoroughly British bout of prolonged indecision. They looked around as if believing in the books, which had been bought by the yard, and the pictures, which were school of Nondescript and So-So; possibly old, possibly not, but ripped untimely from a condemned country house blown up or down, unlamented in the fifties. They were not very good, but depicted people who had once existed just as the authors of the books had once drawn breath. The Club lacked even that humdrum reality but was fake in much the same way as the Swanleys and other suspects. This made them feel at home. Those books that had not been purchased by the yard from the wreck of someone's private library were pure invention. In this category, Bogor identified the *A to Z of Building* by Timothy Dribble and Hermione Pi. On closer inspection of the frontispiece, Dribble and Pi were described

as "Architects to the Aristocracy." Bognor snorted. Aristo-
crats were too stupid to qualify for architects, even ones so
obviously fabricated as Dribble and Pi. For those who were
interested in the reality of reading rather than its appearance,
there were ereaders. In deference to reality, these ereaders
were chained to prevent removal, like the books in the medieval libraries in Hereford or at Merton College. They had
been sprayed with *eau de livre*, which suggested to Bognor
that bookishness was implied, and the water was composed
of stale sweat, old leather, cigar smoke, and alcohol fumes—
probably brandy.

Bognor enjoyed this counterfeit quality, relishing the sham
and professionally preferring the mildly crooked to the honest. He moved in this sham world where nothing was quite
as it seemed and he much preferred the genuinely illusory
like The Club to the second-rate reality of minor schools,
restaurants, and their ilk. Give him pretentious legerdemain
over tatty, tacky reality any day of the week. He liked his
flaws concealed, albeit flamboyantly. This should have meant
that he warmed to the Swanleys, but instead he was repelled.
If confronted with the truth of their subterfuge, they would
not even have blustered but gone quietly muttering clichés
about a fair cop.

On the other hand, what was life but a fabrication? In the
words of the Good Book, you bring nothing in and you take
nothing out. In and it's mewling and puking and nakedness; out and it's probably a box and flames. The point is
that we are all a fabrication. You can believe in nurture or

nature, be a Christian or a Dawkins follower, but we arrive at no one's behest much and we depart when our time is up and the Divine Clockmaker calls us in. "Come in, Number Nine." The point is that it makes no difference whether you are Swanley or a duke, the fourteenth Mr. Wilson or the fortieth Mr. Wilson. The point is that you may get dealt certain cards along the way but essentially you make it up as you go along. The point, the point . . . what was it the man said? "Nothing matters very much, and very little matters at all." Balfour. Tory politician. And if you thought that way, therefore a bad thing. Bognor, on the other hand, considered himself less doctrinaire than that. His was a mind waiting to be made up.

So where did all that leave Swanley? Bognor thought about the Swanley problem and then dismissed him. He had not reached retirement age, nor risen to the head of his department and been honored by Her Majesty in order to bother himself with the likes of Swanley. Though who *were* the likes of Swanley, and was he, Bognor, merely being impossibly snobby and priggish that the likes of Swanley were *Untermensch*? If he really did believe in the nakedness theory—and many did not—then Swanley was as important as he. No more and no less, but just as worthy of consideration. It depended, he supposed, on whether one subscribed to the half-empty or half-full theory of life.

He sighed and wondered where it did leave Swanley and whether it mattered.

Probably not. Prejudice and professionalism did not sit

well together, and though he was both, he had never con-
sciously allowed the former to interfere with the latter, job-
wise. He disliked Swanley personally, but that had nothing to
do with the job in hand.

"Mr. Swanley," he said, shaking the German accountant
by the hand with every manifestation of warmth he did not
feel. "And this must be Mrs. Swanley. How good of you to
come." To himself he was thinking that it was not good; that
they were seldom invited out and were curious.

"Indeed," said Swanley. "Wretched business. Wretched.
Be glad when it's all over. Very."

"Eric's been very poorly ever since it happened. Cough he
can't shake off and not eating properly. I keep telling him that
Mr. Silverburger was only another client, but he won't have it.
Insists he was much more than a client. I tell him he mustn't
let business and pleasure get in each other's way, but he won't
have it. Not Eric. Not the man I married."

"Well, thank you for coming anyway," he said, thinking
unfairly that the Swanleys were fakes among fakes. Even the
orange juice was from a packet. Reconstituted. Only the pea-
nuts were real. The wine might have originally come from
grapes, but it did not come from the country it claimed and
had spent too long in a tanker offshore. All was fake but,
ultimately, did this matter?

Trevor arrived soon after the Swanleys. He was wearing a
mass-produced suit, undertaker-style, and seemed more than
usually deferential. Bognor had trouble working out the Balt.
For a start, although he had never been to either country,

he would have worked out whether he came from Latvia or Lithuania. Trevor seemed to have come from neither and both, simultaneously. Bognor decided he was Estonian. The only Lithuanian actor Bognor could think of was Laurence Harvey, who was so bad he wasn't even a joke. Trevor buttled for Silverburger, enjoyed helping out at tea parties, and aspired to being the next Harvey, thinking he was a famous actor. He could well have been the next L. Harvey. He was definitely bad enough. Bognor suspected Trevor of muddling Olivier with Harvey. It was a common error in un-thespian circles. The only famous Lett Simon could think of was not an actor but the poet, Janis Blodnieks. Simon questioned his first name, which he thought should be Anders, and his poetry. Besides, Blodnieks had been made up by a man named Arnold Harvey. Never mind. Bognor would not have been surprised to find women's clothing in Trevor's wardrobe, but he would have been amazed to find a harlequin's outfit, let alone a crossbow.

"Ah, *Signora Vincent, Signor e Signora Ponti*," Bognor greeted the new arrivals.

"*Signorina*, actually," said Ingrid, who was auntless but had been obviously hitting the gin. Bognor reflected that everything about Ingrid was fake, but so much so, and so obviously, that it came out the other side and he ended up rather liking her. She was so clearly artificial in every respect that you ended up admiring her. She was a flamboyant fake; a positive Cartland, all pink and pancake. So much so that one sometimes forgot that underneath the boa and the makeup there was real flesh and blood and a heart that beat. There was nothing real about Ingrid from her name, age, and nationality to her face, breasts, shoulders, and, above all, her hair. Not just a wig but a bad one.

Bognor found himself warming to Ingrid. This was absurd since she was as false as the other guests and suspects. It was more that she was a lie in which no one could believe. Nor, in a sense, was one supposed to. She was the original fake. Even her sex was dubious. Had she said that she was a drag artist, à Danny la Rue or Dame Edna, one would simply have shrugged and smiled. What she did, however, was to demonstrate that Bognor was not influenced by duplicity. When it came to insincerity, style was vital.

La Vincent had it in spades even though her fakeness was there for all to see.

The Pontis were a different kettle of fish. They intended to deceive, at least in Northamptonshire. They were probably the only people apart from Bognor himself who actually came from their country of origin. Bognor fingered his Apocrypha tie with its improbably garish stripes and laughed thinly. In a number of important other respects, however, they were as much imposters as everyone else. The only reason they had moved to Northants was that Italians were comparatively thin on the ground. Therefore, there were fewer potential whistleblowers there.

None of which explained why he had a soft spot for Ingrid, whoever she might be, and none for the others. He considered the question and decided that liking was not a rational set of beliefs or values. He liked Ingrid and disliked the Swanleys, Trevor the Balt, and the Pontis. He did not need reasons for doing so; indeed, reasons would have been suspicious. Liking was akin to love. It happened at first sight and was often dangerous and unsuitable. Nonetheless, it was real. It happened.

When it came to his job, however, it was irrelevant. If it interfered with his professionalism, it had no place in his personal scheme. He thus afforded precisely the same greeting to Ingrid Vincent as to the others. It happened that he did not believe in the guilt of any of them, but that was not important. All were equally suspicious; each was as potentially culpable as the next. His own personal predilections did not come into the matter. They were private prejudices, and at times like this, he was remorselessly cold-blooded.

Just like a murderer.

That left Benito, the taxi-driving male prostitute; Sophia, his female equivalent; and the priest, Father Carlo. They arrived together, though whether they had set off like that was open to question.

Bognor greeted them, made sure they were all suitably lubricated, and cleared his throat. He was about to begin.

This was as near perfect as it was going to get. Everything was fake, including the suspects. Especially the suspects. Yet its very facsimile quality was part of the attraction. *For what use was the truth to people such as this?* Bognor wondered.

Monica wondered. Contractor wondered. They wondered if the others wondered among the artificial smells and generally fake ambience. Perhaps it did not matter. Metaphorically, Bognor shrugged.

"Thank you all for coming," he said, before beginning a ritual character assassination. He started with the Brits of whom the German-born accountant was first. "I make no secret of my dislike and disbelief in accountancy," he said. "Accountancy is founded on the belief that everything is orderly and runs on time. This is false. I know it. You know it. Life is chaotic and makes little or no sense but accountancy pretends otherwise. Besides which you are a Kraut. This is not your fault, but pretending *is*. We British call that hypocrisy and we do not like it. Besides which, Krauts tend to believe in an eternal timetable. That lie is your problem."

He cleared his throat. "We British believe in chaos. Krauts don't. That's why we won the war. Only we don't mention it. That's another season."

He realized he was reducing Eric Swanley to a stereotype. He said so and apologized. "He is a Kraut accountant. This is as bad as it gets, but it does not mean that he killed Irving Silverburger." He said much the same for the sexy gondolier and the equally sexy hotel maid and the no longer sexy Pupescu. Trevor the Balt might have been sexy but not for the deceased, and by the same token, the Northamptonshire inhabitants who belonged in the pages of "Come Hither" or "I Spy" rather than the English shires. Not for them country life, let alone twin sets and pearls.

It was as he dilated on them that he realized that only one of his suspects had no British base. Was it xenophobia that put Father Carlo where he was? Was he like the new pope, a Jesuit with Franciscan proclivities? Or the other way around? Did this matter? He was inclined to think that nothing much did particularly when he stood where he was—as it were.

He sighed inwardly. Time was when the surroundings would have been real and likewise the suspects who would have been whittled away by a combination of personal forensics and intuition or hunch. Time was. Maybe time had passed him by and all men of his age were similarly perplexed. This he doubted.

In any case, he was not perplexed. Far from it. It was just that he had reached his conclusion by the bludgeon not the rapier, by crudity when he preached and practiced sophistication. He regarded himself as traditionalist yet innovative.

"I am struck," he continued, and extemporizing as he did, "by how many of you have come to Britain. I know that we are in many ways the center of the world and yet Venice . . . and yet Venice . . ." He let the sentence hang, tantalizing for the Balts and East Europeans who, however briefly, had made La Serenissima their home. In his own curious way, he loved the city. The English did. He supposed their tweedy pragmatism thought the place exotic.

"In the words of the man from the BBC, I think you are pretty nasty pieces of work—at best confidence tricksters and at worst liars; and about everything, about life itself. You

would sell your mother or your wife. I on the other hand ...
let's just say that I am on the other hand. And leave it there.
All the same, it doesn't mean that you killed Silverburger,
himself incidentally also a nasty piece of work who left leaving the world a better place. That is irrelevant. It's all irrelevant, I fear. Life's like that. Wish it weren't."

He paused. "So," he resumed, "the Brits didn't do it. You
may be masquerading, but you never dunnit. Fluke. Accident.
Call it what you will, but you did not do it. You could have,
but you had no motive. The reverse, in fact. You may have
been wrong, but your best interests were served by keeping Irving alive. All except one." He repeated the last phrase
partly for effect but partly because it gave him the chance to
decide what to say next. "All except one." He paused—for a
similar combination of reasons.

"Funny thing, religion," he said, then remembered that
many of his audience were foreign and therefore unfamiliar
with English idiom and amended it to "odd thing religion,"
then changed it to what he should have said in the first place.
More alliterative, just as idiomatic; perfect. "Rum thing, religion. True Christians believe there is another life after this
one. If you believe this life is simply a preparation for what
comes later, death is ... well, death has no capacity to inspire
fear. Isn't that so?" He seemed to be musing but was actually
about to pounce.

This he did. "You're a man of God, Father Carlo," he said.
"Wouldn't you agree?" The priest went puce, grinned, and
shook his head. "And there," said Bognor, "I was a silly old

lapsed Anglican, assuming that Carlo, by way of his calling, believed in the afterlife. Ain't necessarily so, which you might think leaves me dead in the water were it not for the reverend gentleman's fondness for dressing up and his interest in ballistics, medieval and other. Would you not agree, Father?" This last query was full of menace, though not perhaps on paper.

Privately, Bognor knew that he had Father Carlo on toast because earlier he had done the unthinkable and organized searches. He hated doing so, for searching implied failure. For much the same reason, he hated calling Michael. He loved hearing his friend's voice but loathed what he was telling him. Message bad, medium good—a something for the late Marshall McLuhan. Victory probably, since victories were gained almost exclusively posthumously.

He sighed inwardly. An outward sigh would give away too much. "Most of you had good reasons for wanting the deceased alive. For Father Carlo, it was a matter of indifference. He didn't care whether Silverburger lived or died. More than that, his whole life was predicated on the belief that there is no difference between what most of us call life and death. But Carlo was curious."

He was anxious to know what effect his words were having. He looked around him and thought of Christopher Wren. *Circumspice.* What need of conventional memorials when you had only to look around his and God's house? Memorial, yes. Conventional, no. He had authorized the British searches personally; Michael, the Italian. He had protested; had argued that this, the dawn breaking-down of doors, the surprise attack was contrary to their life's work. A hatred of such crudity was implicit in their joining up and had informed everything since. Such unarguable arrogance was against justice. The search warrant and all that it implied ran counter to common sense. Bognor agreed but needs must. And pragmatism prevailed.

Truth to tell, Bognor and Dibdini were well past their sell-by date and hopelessly optimistic. The death of Silverburger could probably only have been solved by search warrant or by similar crude and unfair methods. Motive, according to Bognor, was crucial, and yet Father Carlo had no motive. Even Bognor, who liked murderers and even if pushed, approved their crime, hesitated before conceding that lack of conventional motive was part of his "charm" and yet, and yet . . .

Bognor went on out loud, "At dawn, armed and uniformed police searched the unoccupied apartment of Father Carlo Quattrovani of the Frari in Venice. They found and removed one crossbow, one half empty box of ammunition, and one Harlequin's outfit, complete with mask." Bognor stared ahead without expression. "Case rests," he said eventually.

It was a huge case from a publicity point of view, and Carlo's alleged suicide in solitary while awaiting trial was the source of speculation, which would have been—or seemed—endless when newspapers were newspapers and before their attention span dwindled. It was evidence in Britain of Italian fecklessness and perfidy and the Catholic Church's corruption. The general hypocrisy, to which Bognor did not subscribe, was "couldn't happen here, guv."

The trouble—one of many—was that in this worst of all possible worlds it might. It was obviously time for grass and retirement. Monica understood. Maybe Contractor. Perhaps Michael. Father Carlo himself. And Bognor?

Only too well, alas.

THE SIMON BOGNOR MYSTERIES

FROM MYSTERIOUSPRESS.COM
AND OPEN ROAD MEDIA

MYSTERIOUS PRESS.COM

Otto Penzler, owner of the Mysterious Bookshop in Manhattan, founded the Mysterious Press in 1975. Penzler quickly became known for his outstanding selection of mystery, crime, and suspense books, both from his imprint and in his store. The imprint was devoted to printing the best books in these genres, using fine paper and top dust-jacket artists, as well as offering many limited, signed editions.

Now the Mysterious Press has gone digital, publishing ebooks through **MysteriousPress.com**.

MysteriousPress.com offers readers essential noir and suspense fiction, hard-boiled crime novels, and the latest thrillers from both debut authors and mystery masters. Discover classics and new voices, all from one legendary source.

FIND OUT MORE AT
WWW.MYSTERIOUSPRESS.COM

FOLLOW US:
@emysteries and Facebook.com/MysteriousPressCom

MysteriousPress.com is one of a select group of publishing partners of Open Road Integrated Media, Inc.

Open Road Integrated Media is a digital publisher and multimedia content company. Open Road creates connections between authors and their audiences by marketing its ebooks through a new proprietary online platform, which uses premium video content and social media.

CPSIA information can be obtained at www.ICGtesting.com
Printed in the USA
LVOW10s2222091014

408158LV00005B/287/P